PENGUIN BOOKS

THE KITEMAKER

Ruskin Bond's first novel, *The Room on the Roof*, written when he was seventeen, won the John Llewellyn Rhys Memorial Prize in 1957. Since then he has written several novellas (including *Vagrants in the Valley*, *A Flight of Pigeons* and *Delhi Is Not Far*), essays, poems and children's books, many of which have been published by Penguin India. He has also written over 500 short stories and articles that have appeared in a number of magazines and anthologies. He received the Sahitya Akademi Award in 1993 and the Padma Shri in 1999.

Ruskin Bond was born in Kasauli, Himachal Pradesh, and grew up in Jamnagar, Dehradun, Delhi and Shimla. As a young man, he spent four years in the Channel Islands and London. He returned to India in 1955 and has never left the country since. He now lives in Landour, Mussoorie, with his adopted family.

## PENGUIN EVERGREENS

The Penguin Evergreens are collections of classic stories—
fiction and non-fiction—that build on Penguin's original
paperback mission of publishing the best books for everyone
to enjoy. The Evergreens are drawn from Penguin's
wide-ranging list of classics and bestsellers by some of
the most recognized writers in the Indian Subcontinent.

The first list of books is

*The Mark of Vishnu: Stories*, Khushwant Singh
*Building a New India*, A.P.J. Abdul Kalam
*My Experiments with Truth*, M.K. Gandhi
*Feluda: Stories*, Satyajit Ray
*Kabuliwallah: Stories*, Rabindranath Tagore
*Kamasutra: Selections*, Vatsyayana
*The Mahabharata: Droupadi's Marriage and
Other Selections*, Vyasa
*Malgudi: Stories*, R.K. Narayan
*Valmiki Ramayana: The Book of Wilderness*
*The Jungle Book*, Rudyard Kipling
*The Kitemaker: Stories*, Ruskin Bond
*The Quilt: Stories*, Ismat Chughtai
*The Shroud: Stories*, Premchand
*Toba Tek Singh: Stories*, Saadat Hasan Manto

# The Kitemaker

*Stories*

RUSKIN BOND

PENGUIN BOOKS

PENGUIN BOOKS
Published by the Penguin Group
Penguin Books India Pvt. Ltd, 11 Community Centre, Panchsheel Park,
New Delhi 110 017, India
Penguin Group (USA) Inc., 375 Hudson Street, New York, New York 10014, USA
Penguin Group (Canada), 90 Eglinton Avenue East, Suite 700, Toronto,
Ontario, M4P 2Y3, Canada (a division of Pearson Penguin Canada Inc.)
Penguin Books Ltd, 80 Strand, London WC2R 0RL, England
Penguin Ireland, 25 St Stephen's Green, Dublin 2, Ireland
(a division of Penguin Books Ltd)
Penguin Group (Australia), 250 Camberwell Road, Camberwell,
Victoria 3124, Australia (a division of Pearson Australia Group Pty Ltd)
Penguin Group (NZ), 67 Apollo Drive, Rosedale, North Shore 0632,
New Zealand (a division of Pearson New Zealand Ltd)
Penguin Group (South Africa) (Pty) Ltd, 24 Sturdee Avenue, Rosebank,
Johannesburg 2196, South Africa

Penguin Books Ltd, Registered Offices: 80 Strand, London WC2R 0RL, England

This selection first published by Penguin Books India 2011

Copyright © Ruskin Bond 2011

All rights reserved

10 9 8 7 6 5 4 3 2 1

ISBN 9780143415978

Typeset in Sabon Roman by SURYA
Printed at Thomson Press India Ltd, New Delhi

# Contents

# life with father

During my childhood and early boyhood with my father, we were never in one house or dwelling for very long. I think the 'Tennis Bungalow' in Jamnagar (in the grounds of the Ram Vilas Palace) housed us for a couple of years, and that was probably the longest period.

In Jamnagar itself we had at least three abodes—a rambling, leaking old colonial mansion called 'Cambridge House'; a wing of an old palace, the Lal Bagh I think it was called, which was also inhabited by bats and cobras; and the aforementioned 'Tennis Bungalow', a converted sports pavilion which was really quite bright and airy.

I think my father rather enjoyed changing houses, setting up home in completely different surroundings. He loved rearranging rooms too, so that this month's sitting room became next month's bedroom, and so on; furniture would also be moved around quite frequently, somewhat to my mother's irritation, for she liked having things in their familiar places. She had grown up in one abode (her father's Dehra house) whereas my father hadn't remained anywhere for very long. Sometimes he spoke of making a home in Scotland, beside Loch Lomond, but it was only a distant dream.

The only real stability was represented by his stamp collection, and this he carried around in a large tin trunk, for it was an extensive and valuable collection—there was an album for each country he specialized in: Greece, Newfoundland, British possessions in the Pacific, Borneo, Zanzibar, Sierra Leone; these were some of the lands whose stamps he favoured most ...

I did share some of his enthusiasm for stamps, and they gave me a strong foundation in geography and political history, for he went to the trouble of telling me something about the places and people depicted on them—that Pitcairn Island was inhabited largely by mutineers from *H.M.S. Bounty*; that the Solomon Islands were famous for their butterflies; that Britannia still ruled the waves (but only just); that Iraq had a handsome young boy king; that in Zanzibar the Sultan wore a fez; that zebras were exclusive to Kenya, Uganda and Tanganyika; that in America presidents were always changing; and that the handsome young hero on Greek stamps was a Greek god with a sore heel. All this and more, I remember from my stamp-sorting sessions with my father. However, it did not form a bond between him and my mother. She was bored with the whole thing.

*

My earliest memories don't come in any particular order, but most of them pertain to Jamnagar, where we lived until I was five or six years old.

There was the beach at Balachandi, and I remember picking up seashells and wanting to collect them much as my father collected stamps. When the tide was out I went paddling with some of the children from the palace.

*Ruskin Bond*

My father set up a schoolroom for the palace children. It was on the ground floor of a rambling old palace, which had a tower and a room on the top. Sometimes I attended my father's classes more as an observer than a scholar. One day I set off on my own to explore the deserted palace, and ascended some wandering steps to the top, where I found myself in a little room full of tiny stained-glass windows. I took turns at each window pane, looking out at a green or red or yellow world. It was a magical room.

Many years later—almost forty years later, in fact—I wrote a story with this room as its setting. It was called 'The Room of Many Colours' and it had in it a mad princess, a gardener and a snake.

\*

Not all memories are dream-like and idyllic. I witnessed my parents' quarrels from an early age, and later when they resulted in my mother taking off for unknown destinations (unknown to me), I would feel helpless and insecure. My father's hand was always there, and I held it firmly until it was wrenched away by the angel of death.

That early feeling of insecurity was never to leave me, and in adult life, when I witnessed quarrels between people who were close to me, I was always deeply disturbed—more for the children, whose lives were bound to be affected by such emotional discord. But can it be helped? People who marry young, even those who are in love, do not really know each other. The body chemistry may be right but the harmony of two minds is what makes relationships endure.

Words of wisdom from a disappointed bachelor!

I don't suppose I would have written so much about

childhood or even about other children if my own childhood had been all happiness and light. I find that those who have had contended, normal childhoods, seldom remember much about them; nor do they have much insight into the world of children. Some of us are born sensitive. And, if, on top of that, we are pulled about in different directions (both emotionally and physically), we might just end up becoming writers.

No, we don't become writers in schools of creative writing. We become writers before we learn to write. The rest is simply learning how to put it all together.

*

I learnt to read from my father but not in his classroom.

The children were older than me. Four of them were princesses, very attractive, but always clad in buttoned-up jackets and trousers. This was a bit confusing for me, because I had at first taken them for boys. One of them used to pinch my cheeks and hug me. While I thought she was a boy, I rather resented the familiarity. When I discovered she was a girl (I had to be told), I wanted more of it.

I was shy of these boyish princesses, and was to remain shy of girls until I was in my teens.

*

Between Tennis Bungalow and the palace were lawns and flower beds. One of my earliest memories is of picking my way through a forest of flowering cosmos; to a five-year-old they were almost trees, the flowers nodding down at me in friendly invitation.

Since then, the cosmos has been my favourite flower—

fresh, open, uncomplicated—living up to its name, *cosmos*, the universe as an ordered whole. White, purple and rose, they are at its best in each other's company, growing almost anywhere, in the hills or on the plains, in Europe or tropical America. Waving gently in the softest of breezes, they are both sensuous and beyond sensuality. An early influence!

There were of course rose bushes in the palace grounds, kept tidy and trim and looking very like those in the illustrations in my first copy of *Alice in Wonderland*, a well-thumbed edition from which my father often read to me. (Not the Tennial illustrations, something a little softer.) I think I have read *Alice* more often than any other book, with the possible exception of *The Diary of a Nobody*, which I turn to whenever I am feeling a little low. Both books help me to a better appreciation of the absurdities of life.

There were extensive lawns in front of the bungalow, where I could romp around or push my small sister around on a tricycle. She was a backward child, who had been affected by polio and some damage to the brain (having been born prematurely and delivered with the help of forceps), and she was the cross that had to be borne by my parents, together and separately. In spite of her infirmities, Ellen was going to outlive most of us.

\*

Although we lived briefly in other houses, and even for a time in the neighbouring state of Pithadia, Tennis Bungalow was our home for most of the time we were in Jamnagar.

There were several Englishmen working for the Jam Saheb. The port authority was under Commander Bourne, a retired British naval officer. And a large farm (including a turkey farm) was run for the state by a Welsh couple, the Jenkins. I remember the veranda of the Jenkins home, because the side table was always stacked with copies of the humorous weekly, *Punch*, mailed regularly to them from England. I was too small to read *Punch*, but I liked looking at the drawings.

The Bournes had a son who was at school in England, but he had left his collection of comics behind, and these were passed on to me. Thus I made the acquaintance of Korky the Kat, Tiger Tim, Desperate Dan, Our Wullie and other comic-paper heroes of the late thirties.

There was one cinema somewhere in the city, and English-language films were occasionally shown. My first film was very disturbing for me, because the hero was run through with a sword. This was Noel Coward's operetta, *Bitter Sweet*, in which Nelson Eddy and Jennette MacDonald made love in duets. My next film was *Tarzan of the Apes*, in which Johny Weissmuller, the Olympic swimmer, gave Maureen O'Sullivan, pretty and petite, a considerable mauling in their treetop home. But it was to be a few years before I became a movie buff.

Looking up one of my tomes of Hollywood history, I note that *Bitter Sweet* was released in 1940, so that was probably our last year in Jamnagar. My father must have been over forty when he joined the Royal Air Force (RAF), to do his bit for King and country. He may have bluffed his age (he was born in 1896), but perhaps you could enlist in your mid-forties during the War. He was given the rank of pilot officer and assigned to the cipher section of Air Headquarters in New Delhi. So there was a Bond working in Intelligence long before the fictional James arrived on the scene.

The War wasn't going too well for England in 1941, and it wasn't going too well for me either, for I found myself

*Ruskin Bond*

interned in a convent school in the hill station of Mussoorie. I hated it from the beginning. The nuns were strict and unsympathetic; the food was awful (stringy meat boiled with pumpkins); the boys were for the most part dull and unfriendly, the girls too subdued; and the latrines were practically inaccessible. We had to bathe in our underwear, presumably so that the nuns would not be distracted by the sight of our undeveloped sex! I had to endure this place for over a year because my father was being moved around from Calcutta to Delhi to Karachi, and my mother was already engaged in her affair with my future stepfather. At times I thought of running away, but where was I to run?

Picture postcards from my father brought me some cheer. These postcards formed part of Lawson Wood's 'Granpop' series—Granpop being an ape of sorts, who indulged in various human activities, such as attending cocktail parties and dancing to Scottish bagpipes. 'Is this how you feel now that the rains are here?' my father had written under one illustration of Granpop doing the rumba in a tropical downpour.

I enjoyed getting these postcards, with the messages from my father saying that books and toys and stamps were waiting for me when I came home. I preserved them for fifty years, and now they are being looked after by Dr Howard Gotlieb in my archives at Boston University's Mugar Memorial Library. My own letters can perish, but not those postcards!

I have no cherished memories of life at the convent school. It wasn't a cruel place but it lacked character of any kind; it was really a conduit for boys and girls going on to bigger schools in the hill station. I am told that today it has a beautiful well-stocked library, but that the children are not allowed to use the books lest they soil them; everything remains as tidy and spotless as the nuns' habits.

One day in mid-term my mother turned up unexpectedly and withdrew me from the school. I was overjoyed but also a little puzzled by this sudden departure. After all, no one had really taken me seriously when I'd said I hated the place.

Oddly enough, we did not stop in Dehradun at my grandmother's place. Instead my mother took me straight to the railway station and put me on the night train to Delhi. I don't remember if anyone accompanied me—I must have been too young to travel alone—but I remember being met at the Delhi station by my father in full uniform. It was early summer, and he was in khakis, but the blue RAF cap took my fancy. Come winter, he'd be wearing a dark blue uniform with a different kind of cap, and by then he'd be a flying officer and getting saluted by juniors. Being wartime, everyone was saluting madly, and I soon developed the habit, saluting everyone in sight.

An uncle on my mother's side, Fred Clark, was then the station superintendent at Delhi railway station, and he took us home for breakfast to his bungalow, not far from the station. From the conversation that took place during the meal I gathered that my parents had separated, that my mother was remaining in Dehradun, and that henceforth I would be in my father's custody. My sister Ellen was to stay with 'Calcutta Granny'—my father's seventy-year-old mother. The arrangement pleased me, I must admit.

*

The two years I spent with my father were probably the happiest of my childhood—although, for him, they must have been a period of trial and tribulation. Frequent bouts of malaria had undermined his constitution; the separation from my mother weighed heavily on him, and it could not

*Ruskin Bond*

be reversed; and at the age of eight I was self-willed and demanding.

He did his best for me, dear man. He gave me his time, his companionship, his complete attention.

A year was to pass before I was re-admitted to a boarding school, and I would have been quite happy never to have gone to school again. My year in the convent had been sufficient punishment for uncommitted sins. I felt that I had earned a year's holiday.

It was a glorious year, during which we changed our residence at least four times—from a tent on a flat treeless plain outside Delhi, to a hutment near Humayun's tomb; to a couple of rooms on Atul Grove Road; to a small flat on Hailey Road; and finally to an apartment in Scindia House, facing the Connaught Circus.

We were not very long in the tent and hutment—but long enough for me to remember the scorching winds of June, and the *bhisti's* hourly visit to douse the *khas-khas* matting with water. This turned a hot breeze into a refreshing, fragrant zephyr—for about half an hour. And then the dust and the prickly heat took over again. A small table fan was the only luxury.

Except for Sundays, I was alone during most of the day; my father's office in Air Headquarters was somewhere near India Gate. He'd return at about six, tired but happy to find me in good spirits. For although I had no friends during that period, I found plenty to keep me occupied—books, stamps, the old gramophone, hundreds of postcards which he'd collected during his years in England, a scrapbook, albums of photographs ... And sometimes I'd explore the jungle behind the tents; but I did not go very far, because of the snakes that proliferated there.

I would have my lunch with a family living in a neighbouring tent, but at night my father and I would eat together. I forget who did the cooking. But he made the breakfast, getting up early to whip up some fresh butter (he loved doing this) and then laying the table with cornflakes or grapenuts, and eggs poached or fried.

The gramophone was a great companion when my father was away. He had kept all the records he had collected in Jamnagar, and these were added to from time to time. There were operatic arias and duets from *La Bohème* and *Madame Butterfly*; ballads and traditional airs rendered by Paul Robeson, Peter Dawson, Richard Crooks, Webster Booth, Nelson Eddy and other tenors and baritones, and of course the great Russian bass, Chaliapin. And there were lighter, music-hall songs and comic relief provided by Gracie Fields (the 'Lancashire Lass'), George Formy with his ukelele, Arthur Askey ('big-hearted' Arthur—he was a tiny chap), Flanagan and Allan, and a host of other recording artistes. You couldn't just put on some music and lie back and enjoy it. That was the day of the wind-up gramophone, and it had to be wound up fairly vigorously before a 75 rmp record could be played. I enjoyed this chore. The needle, too, had to be changed after almost every record, if you wanted to keep them in decent condition. And the records had to be packed flat, otherwise, in the heat and humidity they were inclined to assume weird shapes and become unplayable.

It was always a delight to accompany my father to one of the record shops in Connaught Place, and come home with a new record by one of our favourite singers.

After a few torrid months in the tent-house and then in a brick hutment, which was even hotter, my father was permitted to rent rooms of his own on Atul Grove Road, a tree-lined lane not far from Connaught Place, which was then the hub and business centre of New Delhi. Keeping me with him had been quite official; his superiors were always wanting to know why my mother wasn't around to look after me. He was really hoping that the war would end soon, so that he could take me to England and put me in a good school there. He had been selling some of his more valuable stamps and had put a bit in the bank.

One evening he came home with a bottle of Scotch whisky. This was most unusual, because I had never seen him drinking—not even beer. Had he suddenly decided to hit the bottle?

The mystery was solved when an American officer dropped in to have dinner with us (having a guest for dinner was a very rare event), and our cook excelled himself by producing succulent pork chops, other viands and vegetables, and my favourite chocolate pudding. Before we sat down for dinner, our guest polished off several pegs of whisky (my father had a drink too), and after dinner they sat down to go through some of my father's stamp albums. The American collector bought several stamps, and we went to bed richer by a couple of thousand rupees.

That it was possible to make money out of one's hobby was something I was to remember when writing became my passion.

When my father had a bad bout of malaria and was admittted to the Military Hospital, I was on my own for about ten days. Our immediate neighbours, an elderly Anglo-Indian couple, kept an eye on me, only complaining that I went through a tin of guava jam in one sitting. This tendency to over-indulge has been with me all my life. Those stringy convent meals must have had something to do with it.

I made one friend during the Atul Grove days. He was a boy called Joseph—from South India, I think—who lived next door. In the evenings we would meet on a strip of grassland across the road and engage in wrestling bouts which were watched by an admiring group of servants' children from a nearby hostelry. We also had a great deal of fun in the trenches that had been dug along the road in case of possible Japanese air raids (there had been one on Calcutta). During the monsoon they filled with rainwater, much to the delight of the local children, who used them as miniature swimming pools. They were then quite impracticable as air raid shelters.

Of course, the real war was being fought in Burma and the Far East, but Delhi was full of men in uniform. When winter came, my father's khakis were changed for dark blue RAF caps and uniforms, which suited him nicely. He was a good-looking man, always neatly dressed; on the short side but quite sturdy. He was over forty when he had joined up—hence the office job, deciphering (or helping to create) codes and ciphers. He was quite secretive about it all (as indeed he was supposed to be), and as he confided in me on almost every subject but his work, he was obviously a reliable Intelligence officer.

He did not have many friends in Delhi. There was the occasional visit to Uncle Fred near the railway station, and sometimes he'd spend a half-hour with Mr Rankin, who owned a large drapery shop at Connaught Circus, where officers' uniforms were tailored. Mr Rankin was another enthusiastic stamp collector, and the two of them would get together in Mr Rankin's back office and exchange stamps or discuss new issues. I think the drapery establishment closed down after the War. Mr Rankin was always extremely well dressed, as though he had stepped straight out of Saville Row and on to the steamy streets of Delhi.

My father and I explored old tombs and monuments, but going to the pictures was what we did most, if he was back from work fairly early.

Connaught Place was well served with cinemas—the Regal, Rivoli, Odeon and Plaza, all very new and shiny— and they exhibited the latest Hollywood and British productions. It was in these cinemas that I discovered the beautiful Sonja Henie, making love on skates and even getting married on ice; Nelson and Jeanette making love in duets; Errol Flynn making love on the high seas; and Gary Cooper and Claudette Colbert making love in the bedroom (*Bluebeard's Eighth Wife*). I made careful listings of all the films I saw, including their casts, and to this day I can give you the main performers in almost any film made in the 1940s. And I still think it was cinema's greatest decade, with the stress on good story, clever and economical direction (films seldom exceeded 120-minutes running time), superb black and white photography, and actors and actresses who were also personalities in their own right. The era of sadistic thrills, gore and psychopathic killers was still far away. The accent was on entertainment— naturally enough, when the worst war in history had spread across Europe, Asia and the Pacific.

*

When my father broached the subject of sending me to a boarding school, I used every argument I could think of to dissuade him. The convent school was still fresh in my memory and I had no wish to return to any institution remotely resembling it—certainly not after almost a year of untrammelled freedom and my father's companionship.

'Why do you want to send me to school again?' I asked. 'I can learn more at home. I can read books, I can write letters, I can even do sums!'

'Not bad for a boy of nine,' said my father. 'But I can't teach you algebra, physics and chemistry.'

'I don't want to be a chemist.'

'Well, what would you like to be when you grow up?'

'A tap-dancer.'

'We've been seeing too many pictures. Everyone says I spoil you.'

I tried another argument. 'You'll have to live on your own again. You'll feel lonely.'

'That can't be helped, son. But I'll come to see you as often as I can. You see, they're posting me to Karachi for some time, and then I'll be moved again—they won't allow me to keep you with me at some of these places. Would you like to stay with your mother?'

I shook my head.

'With Calcutta Granny?'

'I don't know her.'

'When the War's over I'll take you with me to England. But for the next year or two we must stay here. I've found a nice school for you.'

'Another convent?'

'No, it's a prep school for boys in Simla. And I may be able to get posted there during the summer.'

'I want to see it first,' I said.

'We'll go up to Simla together. Not now—in April or May, before it gets too hot. It doesn't matter if you join school a bit later—I know you'll soon catch up with the others.'

There was a brief trip to Dehradun. I think my father felt that there was still a chance of a reconciliation with my mother. But her affair with the businessman was too far gone. His own wife had been practically abandoned and left to look after the photography shop she'd brought along with her dowry. She was a stout lady with high blood pressure, who once went in search of my mother and stepfather with an axe. Fortunately, they were not at home that day and she had to vent her fury on the furniture.

*Ruskin Bond*

In later years, when I got to know her quite well, she told me that my father was a very decent man, who treated her with great courtesy and kindness on the one occasion they met.

I remember we stayed in a little hotel or boarding house just off the Eastern Canal Road.

Dehra was a green and leafy place. The houses were separated by hedges, not walls, and the residential areas were criss-crossed by little lanes bordered by hibiscus or oleander shrubs.

We were soon back in Delhi.

My parents' separation was final and it was to be almost two years before I saw my mother again.

# my father's last letter

1944. The war dragged on. No sooner was I back in prep school than my father was transferred to Calcutta. In some ways this was a good thing because my sister Ellen was there, living with 'Calcutta Granny', and my father could live in his own home for a change. Granny had been living on Park Lane ever since Grandfather had died.

It meant, of course, that my father couldn't come to see me in Simla during my mid-term holidays. But he wrote regularly—once a week, on an average. The War was coming to an end, peace was in the air, but there was also talk of the British leaving India as soon as the war was over. In his letters my father spoke of the preparations he was making towards that end. Obviously he saw no future for us in a free India. He was not an advocate of Empire but he took a pragmatic approach to the problems of the day. There would be a new school for me in England, he said, and meanwhile he was selling off large segments of his stamp collection so that we'd have some money to start life afresh when he left the RAF. There was also his old mother to look after, and my sister Ellen and a baby brother, William, who was to be caught in no-man's land.

I did not concern myself too much with the future. Scout camps at Tara Devi and picnics at the Brockhurst tennis courts were diversions in a round of classes, games, dormitory inspections and evening homework. We could shower in the evenings, a welcome change from the tubs of my former school; and we did not have to cover our nudity—there were no nuns in attendance, only our prefects, who were there to see that we didn't scream the place down.

Did we have sexual adventures? Of course we did. It would have been unreasonable to expect a horde of eight to twelve-year-olds to take no interest in those parts of their anatomy which were undergoing constant change during puberty. But it did not go any further than a little clandestine masturbation in the dormitories late at night. There were no scandals, no passionate affairs, at least none that I can recall. We were at the age of inquisitive and innocent enquiry; not (as yet) the age of emotional attachment or experimentation.

Sex was far down our list of priorities; far behind the exploits of the new comic-book heroes—Captain Marvel, Superman, the Green Lantern and others of their ilk. They had come into the country in the wake of the American troops, and looked like they would stay after everyone had gone. We modelled ourselves on our favourite heroes, giving each other names like Bulletman or Wonderman.

Our exploits, however, did not go far beyond the spectacular pillow-fights that erupted every now and then between the lower and upper dormitories, or one section of a dormitory and another. Those fluffy feather pillows, lovingly stitched together by fond mothers (or the darzi sitting on the veranda), would sometimes come apart, resulting in a storm of feathers sweeping across the dorm. On one occasion, the headmaster's wife, alerted by all the noise, rushed into the dorm, only to be greeted by a feather pillow full in the bosom. Mrs Priestley was a largebosomed woman—we called her breasts 'nutcrackers'—and the pillow burst against them. She slid to the ground, buried in down. As punishment we all received the flat of her hairbrush on our posteriors. Canings were given only in the senior school.

Mrs Priestley played the piano, her husband the violin. They practised together in the assembly hall every evening. They had no children and were not particularly fond of children, as far as I could tell. In fact, Mrs Priestley had a positive antipathy for certain boys and lost no opportunity in using her brush on them. Mr Priestley showed a marked preference for upper-class English boys, of whom there were a few. He was lower middle class himself (as I discovered later).

Some good friends and companions during my two-and-a-half prep school years were Peter Blake, who did his hair in a puff like Alan Ladd; Brian Abbott, a quite boy who boasted only of his father's hunting exploits—Abbott was a precursor to Jim Corbett, but never wrote anything; Riaz Khan, a good-natured, fun-loving boy; and Bimal Mirchandani, who grew up to become a Bombay industrialist. I don't know what happened to the others.

As I have said, I kept my father's letters, but the only one that I was able to retain (apart from some of the postcards) was the last one, which I reproduce here.

It is a good example of the sort of letter he wrote to me, and you can see why I hung on to it.

AA Bond 108485 (RAF)<br>
c/o 231 Group<br>
Rafpost<br>
Calcutta 20/8/44

My dear Ruskin,

Thank you very much for your letter received a few days ago. I was pleased to hear that you were quite well and learning hard. We are all quite O.K. here, but I am still not strong enough to go to work after the recent attack of malaria I had. I was in hospital for a long time and that is the reason why you did not get a letter from me for several weeks.

I have now to wear glasses for reading, but I do not use them for ordinary wear—but only when I read or do book work. Ellen does not wear glasses at all now.

Do you need any new warm clothes? Your warm suits must be getting too small. I am glad to hear the rains are practically over in the hills where you are. It will be nice to have sunny days in September when your holidays are on. Do the holidays begin from the 9th of Sept? What will you do? Is there to be Scouts Camp at Taradevi? Or will you catch butterflies on sunny days on the school Cricket Ground? I am glad to hear you have lots of friends. Next year you will be in the top class of the Prep. School. You only have 3½ months more for the Xmas holidays to come round, when you will be glad to come home, I am sure, to do more Stamp work and Library Study. The New Market is full of book shops here. Ellen loves the market.

I wanted to write before about your writing Ruskin, but forgot. Sometimes I get letters from you written in very small handwriting, as if you wanted to squeeze a lot of news into one sheet of letter paper. It is not good for you or for your eyes, to get into the habit of writing small. I know your handwriting is good and that you came 1st in class for handwriting, but try and form a larger style of writing and do not worry if you can't get all your news into one sheet of paper—but stick to big letters.

We have had a very wet month just passed. It is still cloudy, at night we have to use fans, but during the cold weather it is nice—not too cold like Delhi and not too warm either—but just moderate. Granny is quite well. She and Ellen send you their fond love. The last I heard a week ago, that William and all at Dehra were well also.

We have been without a cook for the past few days. I hope we find a good one before long. There are not many. I wish I could get our Delhi cook, the old man now famous for his 'Black Puddings' which Ellen hasn't seen since we arrived in Calcutta 4 months ago.

I have still got the Records and Gramophone and most of the best books, but as they are all getting old and some not suited to you which are only for children under 8 yrs old—I will give some to William, and Ellen and you can buy some new ones when you come home for Xmas. I am re-arranging all the stamps that became loose and topsy-turvy after people came and went through the collections to buy stamps. A good many got sold, the rest got mixed up a bit and it is now taking up all my time putting the balance of the collection in order. But as I am at home all day, unable to go to work as yet, I have lots of time to finish the work of re-arranging the Collection. Ellen loves drawing. I give her paper and a pencil and let her draw for herself without any help, to get her used to holding paper and pencil. She has got expert at using her pencil now and draws some wonderful animals like camels, elephants, dragons with many heads—cobras—rain clouds shedding buckets of water—tigers with long grass around them—horses with manes and wolves and foxes with bushy hair. Sometimes you can't see much of the animals because there is too much grass covering them or too much hair on the foxes and wolves and too much mane on the horses' necks—or too much rain from the clouds. All this decoration is made up by a sort of heavy scribbling of lines, but through it all one can see some very good shapes of animals, elephants and ostriches and other things. I will send you some.

*Ruskin Bond*

Well, Ruskin, I hope this finds you well. With fond love from us all. Write again soon. Ever your loving daddy ...

*

It was about two weeks after receiving this letter that I was given the news of my father's death. Those frequent bouts of malaria had undermined his health, and a severe attack of jaundice did the rest. A kind but inept teacher, Mr Murtough, was given the unenviable task of breaking the news to me. He mumbled something about God needing my father more than I did, and of course I knew what had happened and broke down and had to be taken to the infirmary, where I remained for a couple of days. It never made any sense to me why God should have needed my father more than I did, unless of course He envied my father's stamp collection. If God was Love, why did He have to break up the only loving relationship I'd known so far? What would happen to me now, I wondered ... would I live with Calcutta Granny or some other relative or be put away in an orphanage?

Mr Priestley saw me in his office and said I'd be going to my mother when school closed. He said he'd been told that I had kept my father's letters and that if I wished to put them in his safe keeping he'd see that they were not lost. I handed them over—all except the one I've reproduced here.

The day before we broke up for the school holidays, I went to Mr Priestley and asked for my letters. 'What letters?' He looked bemused, irritated. He'd had a trying day. 'My father's letters,' I told him. 'You said you'd keep them for me.' 'Did I? Don't remember. Why should I want to keep your father's letters?' 'I don't know, sir. You put them in your drawer.' He opened the drawer, shut it.

'None of your letters here. I'm very busy now, Bond. If I find any of your letters, I'll give them to you.' I was dismissed from his presence.

I never saw those letters again. And I'm glad to say I did not see Mr Priestley again. All he'd given me was a lifelong aversion to violin players.

# untouchable

The sweeper boy splashed water over the *khus* matting
that hung in the doorway and for a while the air was
cooled.

I sat on the edge of my bed, staring out of the open
window, brooding upon the dusty road shimmering in the
noon-day heat. A car passed and the dust rose in billowing
clouds.

Across the road lived the people who were supposed to
look after me while my father lay in hospital with malaria.
I was supposed to stay with them, sleep with them. But
except for meals, I kept away. I did not like them and they
did not like me.

For a week, longer probably, I was going to live alone in
the red-brick bungalow on the outskirts of the town, on
the fringe of the jungle. At night the sweeper boy would
keep guard, sleeping in the kitchen. Apart from him, I had
no company; only the neighbours' children, and I did not
like them and they did not like me.

Their mother said, 'Don't play with the sweeper boy, he
is unclean. Don't touch him. Remember, he is a servant.
You must come and play with my boys.'

Well, I did not intend playing with the sweeper boy ... but neither did I intend playing with her children. I was going to sit on my bed all week and wait for my father to come home.

Sweeper boy ... all day he pattered up and down between the house and the water-tank, with the bucket clanging against his knees.

Back and forth, with a wide, friendly smile.

I frowned at him.

He was about my age, ten. He had short-cropped hair, very white teeth, and muddy feet, hands, and face. All he wore was an old pair of khaki shorts; the rest of his body was bare, burnt a deep brown.

At every trip to the water tank he bathed, and returned dripping and glistening from head to toe.

I dripped with sweat.

It was supposedly below my station to bathe at the tank, where the gardener, water carrier, cooks, ayahs, sweepers, and their children all collected. I was the son of a 'sahib' and convention ruled that I did not play with servant children.

But I was just as determined not to play with the other sahibs' children, for I did not like them and they did not like me.

I watched the flies buzzing against the windowpane, the lizards scuttling across the rafters, the wind scattering petals of scorched, long-dead flowers.

The sweeper boy smiled and saluted in play. I avoided his eyes and said, 'Go away.'

He went into the kitchen.

I rose and crossed the room, and lifted my sun helmet off the hatstand.

A centipede ran down the wall, across the floor.

I screamed and jumped on the bed, shouting for help.

*Ruskin Bond*

The sweeper boy darted in. He saw me on the bed, the centipede on the floor; and picking a large book off the shelf, slammed it down on the repulsive insect.

I remained standing on my bed, trembling with fear and revulsion.

He laughed at me, showing his teeth, and I blushed and said, 'Get out!'

I would not, could not, touch or approach the hat or hatstand. I sat on the bed and longed for my father to come home.

A mosquito passed close by me and sang in my ear. Half-heartedly, I clutched at it and missed; and it disappeared behind the dressing-table.

That mosquito, I reasoned, gave the malaria to my father. And now it was trying to give it to me!

The next-door lady walked through the compound and smiled thinly from outside the window. I glared back at her.

The sweeper boy passed with the bucket, and grinned. I turned away.

In bed at night, with the lights on, I tried reading. But even books could not quell my anxiety.

The sweeper boy moved about the house, bolting doors, fastening windows. He asked me if I had any orders.

I shook my head.

He skipped across to the electric switch, turned off the light, and slipped into his quarters. Outside, inside, all was dark; only one shaft of light squeezed in through a crack in the sweeper boy's door, and then that too went out.

I began to wish I had stayed with the neighbours. The darkness worried me—silent and close—silent, as if in suspense.

Once a bat flew flat against the window, falling to the ground outside; once an owl hooted. Sometimes a dog barked. And I tautened as a jackal howled hideously in the jungle behind the bungalow. But nothing could break the overall stillness, the night's silence . . .

Only a dry puff of wind . . .

It rustled in the trees, and put me in mind of a snake slithering over dry leaves and twigs. I remembered a tale I had been told not long ago, of a sleeping boy who had been bitten by a cobra.

I would not, could not, sleep. I longed for my father . . .

The shutters rattled, the doors creaked. It was a night for ghosts.

Ghosts!

God, why did I have to think of them?

My God! There, standing by the bathroom door . . .

My father! My father dead from the malaria, and come to see me!

I threw myself at the switch. The room lit up. I sank down on the bed in complete exhaustion, the sweat soaking my nightclothes.

It was not my father I had seen. It was his dressing gown hanging on the bathroom door. It had not been taken with him to the hospital.

I turned off the light.

The hush outside seemed deeper, nearer. I remembered the centipede, the bat, thought of the cobra and the sleeping boy; pulled the sheet tight over my head. If I could see nothing, well then, nothing could see me.

A thunderclap shattered the brooding stillness.

A streak of lightning forked across the sky, so close that even through the sheet I saw a tree and the opposite house silhouetted against the flashing canvas of gold.

I dived deeper beneath the bedclothes, gathered the pillow about my ears.

But at the next thunderclap, louder this time, louder

than I had ever heard, I leapt from my bed. I could not stand it. I fled, blundering into the sweeper boy's room.

The boy sat on the bare floor.

'What is happening?' he asked.

The lightning flashed, and his teeth and eyes flashed with it. Then he was a blur in the darkness.

'I am afraid,' I said.

I moved towards him and my hand touched a cold shoulder.

'Stay here,' he said. 'I too am afraid.'

I sat down, my back against the wall; beside the untouchable, the outcaste . . . and the thunder and lightning ceased, and the rain came down, swishing and drumming on the corrugated roof.

'The rainy season has started,' observed the sweeper boy, turning to me. His smile played with the darkness, and then he laughed. And I laughed too, but feebly.

But I was happy and safe. The scent of the wet earth blew in through the skylight and the rain fell harder.

# the photograph

I was ten years old. My grandmother sat on the string
bed under the mango tree. It was late summer and there
were sunflowers in the garden and a warm wind in the
trees. My grandmother was knitting a woollen scarf for the
winter months. She was very old, dressed in a plain white
sari. Her eyes were not very strong now but her fingers
moved quickly with the needles and the needles kept
clicking all afternoon. Grandmother had white hair but
there were very few wrinkles on her skin.

I had come home after playing cricket on the maidan. I
had taken my meal and now I was rummaging through a
box of old books and family heirlooms that had just that
day been brought out of the attic by my mother. Nothing
in the box interested me very much except for a book with
colourful pictures of birds and butterflies. I was going
through the book, looking at the pictures, when I found a
small photograph between the pages. It was a faded picture,
a little yellow and foggy. It was the picture of a girl
standing against a wall and behind the wall there was
nothing but sky. But from the other side a pair of hands

reached up, as though someone was going to climb the wall. There were flowers growing near the girl but I couldn't tell what they were. There was a creeper too but it was just a creeper.

I ran out into the garden. 'Granny!' I shouted. 'Look at this picture! I found it in the box of old things. Whose picture is it?'

I jumped on the bed beside my grandmother and she walloped me on the bottom and said, 'Now I've lost count of my stitches and the next time you do that I'll make you finish the scarf yourself.'

Granny was always threatening to teach me how to knit which I thought was a disgraceful thing for a boy to do. It was a good deterrent for keeping me out of mischief. Once I had torn the drawing-room curtains and Granny had put a needle and thread in my hand and made me stitch the curtain together, even though I made long, two-inch stitches, which had to be taken out by my mother and done again.

She took the photograph from my hand and we both stared at it for quite a long time. The girl had long, loose hair and she wore a long dress that nearly covered her ankles, and sleeves that reached her wrists, and there were a lot of bangles on her hands. But despite all this drapery, the girl appeared to be full of freedom and movement. She stood with her legs apart and her hands on her hips and had a wide, almost devilish smile on her face.

'Whose picture is it?' I asked.

'A little girl's, of course,' said Grandmother. 'Can't you tell?'

'Yes, but did you know the girl?'

'Yes, I knew her,' said Granny, 'but she was a very wicked girl and I shouldn't tell you about her. But I'll tell you about the photograph. It was taken in your grandfather's house about sixty years ago. And that's the garden wall and over the wall there was a road going to town.'

'Whose hands are they,' I asked, 'coming up from the other side?'

Grandmother squinted and looked closely at the picture, and shook her head. 'It's the first time I've noticed,' she said. 'They must have been the sweeper boy's. Or maybe they were your grandfather's.'

'They don't look like Grandfather's hands,' I said. 'His hands are all bony.'

'Yes, but this was sixty years ago.'

'Didn't he climb up the wall after the photo?'

'No, nobody climbed up. At least, I don't remember.'

'And you remember well, Granny.'

'Yes, I remember ... I remember what is not in the photograph. It was a spring day and there was a cool breeze blowing, nothing like this. Those flowers at the girl's feet, they were marigolds, and the bougainvillea creeper, it was a mass of purple. You cannot see these colours in the photo and even if you could, as nowadays, you wouldn't be able to smell the flowers or feel the breeze.'

'And what about the girl?' I said. 'Tell me about the girl.'

'Well, she was a wicked girl,' said Granny. 'You don't know the trouble they had getting her into those fine clothes she's wearing.'

'I think they are terrible clothes,' I said.

'So did she. Most of the time, she hardly wore a thing. She used to go swimming in a muddy pool with a lot of ruffianly boys, and ride on the backs of buffaloes. No boy ever teased her, though, because she could kick and scratch and pull his hair out!'

'She looks like it too,' I said. 'You can tell by the way she's smiling. At any moment something's going to happen.'

*Ruskin Bond*

'Something did happen,' said Granny. 'Her mother wouldn't let her take off the clothes afterwards, so she went swimming in them and lay for half an hour in the mud.'

I laughed heartily and Grandmother laughed too.

'Who was the girl?' I said. 'You must tell me who she was.'

'No, that wouldn't do,' said Grandmother, but I pretended I didn't know. I knew, because Grandmother still smiled in the same way, even though she didn't have as many teeth.

'Come on, Granny,' I said, 'tell me, tell me.'

But Grandmother shook her head and carried on with the knitting. And I held the photograph in my hand looking from it to my grandmother and back again, trying to find points in common between the old lady and the little pig-tailed girl. A lemon-coloured butterfly settled on the end of Grandmother's knitting needle and stayed there while the needles clicked away. I made a grab at the butterfly and it flew off in a dipping flight and settled on a sunflower.

'I wonder whose hands they were,' whispered Grandmother to herself, with her head bowed, and her needles clicking away in the soft, warm silence of that summer afternoon.

# the boy who broke the bank

Nathu grumbled to himself as he swept the steps of the Pipalnagar Bank, owned by Seth Govind Ram. He used the small broom hurriedly and carelessly, and the dust, after rising in a cloud above his head, settled down again on the steps. As Nathu was banging his pan against a dustbin, Sitaram, the washerman's son, passed by.

Sitaram was on his delivery round. He had a bundle of freshly pressed clothes balanced on his head.

'Don't raise such dust!' he called out to Nathu. 'Are you annoyed because they are still refusing to pay you an extra two rupees a month?'

'I don't wish to talk about it,' complained the sweeper boy. 'I haven't even received my regular pay. And this is the twentieth of the month. Who would think a bank would hold up a poor man's salary? As soon as I get my money, I'm off! Not another week do I work in this place.' And Nathu banged the pan against the dustbin several times, just to emphasize his point and give himself confidence.

'Well, I wish you luck,' said Sitaram. 'I'll keep a lookout

for any jobs that might suit you.' And he plodded barefoot along the road, the big bundle of clothes hiding most of his head and shoulders.

At the fourth home he visited, Sitaram heard the lady of the house mention that she was in need of a sweeper. Tying his bundle together, he said, 'I know of a sweeper boy who's looking for work. He can start from next month. He's with the bank just now but they aren't giving him his pay, and he wants to leave.'

'Is that so?' said Mrs Srivastava. 'Well, tell him to come and see me tomorrow.'

And Sitaram, glad that he had been of service to both a customer and his friend, hoisted his bag on his shoulders and went his way.

Mrs Srivastava had to do some shopping. She gave instructions to the ayah about looking after the baby, and told the cook not to be late with the midday meal. Then she set out for the Pipalnagar marketplace, to make her customary tour of the cloth shops.

A large, shady tamarind tree grew at one end of the bazaar, and it was here that Mrs Srivastava found her friend Mrs Bhushan sheltering from the heat. Mrs Bhushan was fanning herself with a large handkerchief. She complained of the summer which, she affirmed, was definitely the hottest in the history of Pipalnagar. She then showed Mrs Srivastava a sample of the cloth she was going to buy, and for five minutes they discussed its shade, texture and design. Having exhausted this topic, Mrs Srivastava said, 'Do you know, my dear, that Seth Govind Ram's bank can't even pay its employees? Only this morning I heard a complaint from their sweeper, who hasn't received his wages for over a month!'

'Shocking!' remarked Mrs Bhushan. 'If they can't pay the sweeper they must be in a bad way. None of the others could be getting paid either.'

She left Mrs Srivastava at the tamarind tree and went in search of her husband, who was sitting in front of Kamal Kishore's photographic shop, talking to the owner.

'So there you are!' cried Mrs Bhushan. 'I've been looking for you for almost an hour. Where did you disappear?'

'Nowhere,' replied Mr Bhushan. 'Had you remained stationary in one shop, I might have found you. But you go from one shop to another, like a bee in a flower garden.'

'Don't start grumbling. The heat is trying enough. I don't know what's happening to Pipalnagar. Even the bank's about to go bankrupt.'

'What's that?' said Kamal Kishore, sitting up suddenly. 'Which bank?'

'Why the Pipalnagar Bank, of course. I hear they have stopped paying employees. Don't tell me you have an account there, Mr Kishore?'

'No, but my neighbour has!' he exclaimed; and he called out over the low partition to the keeper of the barber shop next door. 'Deep Chand, have you heard the latest? The Pipalnagar Bank is about to collapse. You better get your money out as soon as you can!'

Deep Chand, who was cutting the hair of an elderly gentleman, was so startled that his hand shook and he nicked his customer's right ear. The customer yelped in pain and distress: pain, because of the cut, and distress, because of the awful news he had just heard. With one side of his neck still unshaven, he sped across the road to the general merchant's store where there was a telephone. He dialled Seth Govind Ram's number. The Seth was not at home. Where was he, then? The Seth was holidaying in Kashmir. Oh, was that so? The elderly gentleman did not believe it. He hurried back to the barber's shop and told Deep Chand: 'The bird has flown! Seth Govind Ram has left town. Definitely, it means a collapse.' And then he

*Ruskin Bond*

dashed out of the shop, making a beeline for his office and chequebook.

The news spread through the bazaar with the rapidity of forest fire. At the general merchant's it circulated amongst the customers, and then spread with them in various directions, to the betel seller, the tailor, the free vendor, the jeweller, the beggar sitting on the pavement.

Old Ganpat, the beggar, had a crooked leg. He had been squatting on the pavement for years, calling for alms. In the evening someone would come with a barrow and take him away. He had never been known to walk. But now, on learning that the bank was about to collapse, Ganpat astonished everyone by leaping to his feet and actually running at top speed in the direction of the bank. It soon became known that he had a thousand rupees in savings!

Men stood in groups at street corners discussing the situation. Pipalnagar seldom had a crisis, seldom or never had floods, earthquakes or drought; and the imminent crash of the Pipalnagar Bank set everyone talking and speculating and rushing about in a frenzy. Some boasted of their farsightedness, congratulating themselves on having already taken out their money, or on never having put any in; others speculated on the reasons for the crash, putting it all down to excesses indulged in by Seth Govind Ram. The Seth had fled the state, said one. He had fled the country, said another. He was hiding in Pipalnagar, said a third. He had hanged himself from the tamarind tree, said a fourth, and had been found that morning by the sweeper boy.

By noon the small bank had gone through all its ready cash, and the harassed manager was in a dilemma. Emergency funds could only be obtained from another bank some thirty miles distant, and he wasn't sure he could persuade the crowd to wait until then. And there was no way of contacting Seth Govind Ram on his houseboat in Kashmir.

People were turned back from the counters and told to return the following day. They did not like the sound of that. And so they gathered outside, on the steps of the bank, shouting, 'Give us our money or we'll break in!' and 'Fetch the Seth, we know he's hiding in a safe deposit locker!' Mischief makers who didn't have a paisa in the bank joined the crowd and aggravated the mood. The manager stood at the door and tried to placate them. He declared that the bank had plenty of money but no immediate means of collecting it; he urged them to go home and come back the next day.

'We want it now!' chanted some of the crowd. 'Now, now, now!'

And a brick hurtled through the air and crashed through the plate glass window of the Pipalnagar Bank.

Nathu arrived next morning to sweep the steps of the bank. He saw the refuse and the broken glass and the stones cluttering the steps. Raising his hands in a gesture of horror and disgust he cried: 'Hooligans! Sons of donkeys! As though it isn't bad enough to be paid late, it seems my work has also to be increased!' He smote the steps with his broom scattering the refuse.

'Good morning, Nathu,' said the washerman's boy, getting down from his bicycle. 'Are you ready to take up a new job from the first of next month? You'll have to I suppose, now that the bank is going out of business.'

'How's that?' said Nathu.

'Haven't you heard? Well, you'd better wait here until half the population of Pipalnagar arrives to claim their money.' And he waved cheerfully—he did not have a bank account—and sped away on his cycle.

Nathu went back to sweeping the steps, muttering to

himself. When he had finished his work, he sat down on the highest step, to await the arrival of the manager. He was determined to get his pay.

'Who would have thought the bank would collapse!' he said to himself, and looked thoughtfully into the distance. 'I wonder how it could have happened . . .'

# the fight

R anji had been less than a month in Rajpur when he discovered the pool in the forest. It was the height of summer, and his school had not yet opened, and, having as yet made no friends in this semi-hill station, he wandered about a good deal by himself into the hills and forests that stretched away interminably on all sides of the town. It was hot, very hot, at that time of year, and Ranji walked about in his vest and shorts, his brown feet white with the chalky dust that flew up from the ground. The earth was parched, the grass brown, the trees listless, hardly stirring, waiting for a cool wind or a refreshing shower of rain.

It was on such a day—a hot, tired day—that Ranji found the pool in the forest. The water had a gentle translucency, and you could see the smooth round pebbles at the bottom of the pool. A small stream emerged from a cluster of rocks to feed the pool. During the monsoon, this stream would be a gushing torrent, cascading down from the hills, but during the summer it was barely a trickle. The rocks, however, held the water in the pool, and it did not dry up like the pools in the plains.

When Ranji saw the pool, he did not hesitate to get into it. He had often gone swimming, alone or with friends, when he had lived with his parents in a thirsty town in the middle of the Rajputana desert. There, he had known only sticky, muddy pools, where buffaloes wallowed and women washed clothes. He had never seen a pool like this—so clean and cold and inviting. He threw off all his clothes, as he had done when he went swimming in the plains, and leapt into the water. His limbs were supple, free of any fat, and his dark body glistened in patches of sunlit water.

The next day he came again to quench his body in the cool waters of the forest pool. He was there for almost an hour, sliding in and out of the limpid green water, or lying stretched out on the smooth yellow rocks in the shade of broad-leaved sal trees. It was while he lay thus, naked on a rock, that he noticed another boy standing a little distance away, staring at him in a rather hostile manner. The other boy was a little older than Ranji, taller, thick-set, with a broad nose and thick, red lips. He had only just noticed Ranji, and he stood at the edge of the pool, wearing a pair of bathing shorts, waiting for Ranji to explain himself.

When Ranji did not say anything, the other called out, 'What are you doing here, Mister?'

Ranji, who was prepared to be friendly, was taken aback at the hostility of the other's tone.

'I am swimming,' he replied. 'Why don't you join me?'

'I always swim alone,' said the other. 'This is my pool, I did not invite you here. And why are you not wearing any clothes?'

'It is not your business if I do not wear clothes. I have nothing to be ashamed of.'

'You skinny fellow, put on your clothes.'

'Fat fool, take yours off.'

This was too much for the stranger to tolerate. He strode up to Ranji, who still sat on the rock and, planting his broad feet firmly on the sand, said (as though this would settle the matter once and for all), 'Don't you know I am a Punjabi? I do not take replies from villagers like you!'

'So you like to fight with villagers?' said Ranji. 'Well, I am not a villager. I am a Rajput!'

'I am a Punjabi!'

'I am a Rajput!'

They had reached an impasse. One had said he was a Punjabi, the other had proclaimed himself a Rajput. There was little else that could be said.

'You understand that I am a Punjabi?' said the stranger, feeling that perhaps this information had not penetrated Ranji's head.

'I have heard you say it three times,' replied Ranji.

'Then why are you not running away?'

'I am waiting for *you* to run away!'

'I will have to beat you,' said the stranger, assuming a violent attitude, showing Ranji the palm of his hand.

'I am waiting to see you do it,' said Ranji.

'You will see me do it,' said the other boy.

Ranji waited. The other boy made a strange, hissing sound. They stared each other in the eye for almost a minute. Then the Punjabi boy slapped Ranji across the face with all the force he could muster. Ranji staggered, feeling quite dizzy. There were thick red finger marks on his cheek.

'There you are!' exclaimed his assailant. 'Will you be off now?'

For answer, Ranji swung his arm up and pushed a hard, bony fist into the other's face.

And then they were at each other's throats, swaying on the rock, tumbling on to the sand, rolling over and over, their legs and arms locked in a desperate, violent struggle. Gasping and cursing, clawing and slapping, they rolled right into the shallows of the pool.

Even in the water the fight continued as, spluttering and covered with mud, they groped for each other's head and throat. But after five minutes of frenzied, unscientific struggle, neither boy had emerged victorious. Their bodies heaving with exhaustion, they stood back from each other, making tremendous efforts to speak.

'Now—now do you realize—I am a Punjabi?' gasped the stranger.

'Do you know I am a Rajput?' said Ranji with difficulty.

They gave a moment's consideration to each other's answers, and in that moment of silence there was only their heavy breathing and the rapid beating of their hearts.

'Then you will not leave the pool?' said the Punjabi boy.

'I will not leave it,' said Ranji.

'Then we shall have to continue the fight,' said the other.

'All right,' said Ranji.

But neither boy moved, neither took the initiative.

The Punjabi boy had an inspiration.

'We will continue the fight tomorrow,' he said. 'If you dare to come here again tomorrow, we will continue this fight, and I will not show you mercy as I have done today.'

'I will come tomorrow,' said Ranji. 'I will be ready for you.'

They turned from each other then and, going to their respective rocks, put on their clothes, and left the forest by different routes.

When Ranji got home, he found it difficult to explain the cuts and bruises that showed on his face, legs and arms. It was difficult to conceal the fact that he had been in an unusually violent fight, and his mother insisted on his staying at home for the rest of the day. That evening, though, he slipped out of the house and went to the bazaar, where he found comfort and solace in a bottle of vividly coloured lemonade and a banana leaf full of hot, sweet jalebis. He had just finished the lemonade when he saw his adversary coming down the road. His first impulse was to turn away and look elsewhere, his second to throw the lemonade bottle at his enemy. But he did neither of these things. Instead, he stood his ground and scowled at his passing adversary. And the Punjabi boy said nothing either, but scowled back with equal ferocity.

The next day was as hot as the previous one. Ranji felt weak and lazy and not at all eager for a fight. His body was stiff and sore after the previous day's encounter. But he could not refuse the challenge. Not to turn up at the pool would be an acknowledgement of defeat. From the way he felt just then, he knew he would be beaten in another fight. But he could not acquiesce in his own defeat. He must defy his enemy to the last, or outwit him, for only then could he gain his respect. If he surrendered now, he would be beaten for all time; but to fight and be beaten today left him free to fight and be beaten again. As long as he fought, he had a right to the pool in the forest.

He was half hoping that the Punjabi boy would have forgotten the challenge, but these hopes were dashed when he saw his opponent sitting, stripped to the waist, on a rock on the other side of the pool. The Punjabi boy was rubbing oil on his body, massaging it into his broad thighs. He saw Ranji beneath the sal trees, and called a challenge across the waters of the pool.

'Come over on this side and fight!' he shouted.

But Ranji was not going to submit to any conditions laid down by his opponent.

'Come *this* side and fight!' he shouted back with equal vigour.

*Ruskin Bond*

'Swim across and fight me here!' called the other. 'Or perhaps you cannot swim the length of this pool?'

But Ranji could have swum the length of the pool a dozen times without tiring, and here he would show the Punjabi boy his superiority. So, slipping out of his vest and shorts, he dived straight into the water, cutting through it like a knife, and surfaced with hardly a splash. The Punjabi boy's mouth hung open in amazement.

'You can dive!' he exclaimed.

'It is easy,' said Ranji, treading water, waiting for a further challenge. 'Can't you dive?'

'No,' said the other. 'I jump straight in. But if you will tell me how, I will make a dive.'

'It is easy,' said Ranji. 'Stand on the rock, stretch your arms out and allow your head to displace your feet.'

The Punjabi boy stood up, stiff and straight, stretched out his arms, and threw himself into the water. He landed flat on his belly, with a crash that sent the birds screaming out of the trees.

Ranji dissolved into laughter.

'Are you trying to empty the pool?' he asked, as the Punjabi boy came to the surface, spouting water like a small whale.

'Wasn't it good?' asked the boy, evidently proud of his feat.

'Not very good,' said Ranji. 'You should have more practice. See, I will do it again.'

And pulling himself up on a rock, he executed another perfect dive. The other boy waited for him to come up, but, swimming under water, Ranji circled him and came upon him from behind.

'How did you do that?' asked the astonished youth.

'Can't you swim under water?' asked Ranji.

'No, but I will try it.'

The Punjabi boy made a tremendous effort to plunge to the bottom of the pool and indeed he thought he had gone right down, though his bottom, like a duck's, remained above the surface.

Ranji, however, did not discourage him.

'It was not bad,' he said. 'But you need a lot of practice.'

'Will you teach me?' asked his enemy.

'If you like, I will teach you.'

'You must teach me. If you do not teach me, I will beat you. Will you come here every day and teach me?'

'If you like,' said Ranji. They had pulled themselves out of the water, and were sitting side by side on a smooth grey rock.

'My name is Suraj,' said the Punjabi boy. 'What is yours?'

'It is Ranji.'

'I am strong, am I not?' asked Suraj, bending his arm so that a ball of muscle stood up stretching the white of his flesh.

'You are strong,' said Ranji. 'You are a real *pahelwan*.'

'One day I will be the world's champion wrestler,' said Suraj, slapping his thighs, which shook with the impact of his hand. He looked critically at Ranji's hard thin body. 'You are quite strong yourself,' he conceded. 'But you are too bony. I know, you people do not eat enough. You must come and have your food with me. I drink one *seer* of milk every day. We have got our own cow! Be my friend, and I will make you a pahelwan like me! I know— if you teach me to dive and swim underwater, I will make you a pahelwan! That is fair, isn't it?'

'That is fair!' said Ranji, though he doubted if he was getting the better of the exchange.

Suraj put his arm around the younger boy and said, 'We are friends now, yes?'

They looked at each other with honest, unflinching eyes, and in that moment love and understanding were born.

'We are friends,' said Ranji.

The birds had settled again in their branches, and the pool was quiet and limpid in the shade of the sal trees.

'It is our pool,' said Suraj. 'Nobody else can come here without our permission. Who would dare?'

'Who would dare?' said Ranji, smiling with the knowledge that he had won the day.

# love is a sad song

I sit against this grey rock, beneath a sky of pristine blueness, and think of you, Sushila. It is November and the grass is turning brown and yellow. Crushed, it still smells sweet. The afternoon sun shimmers on the oak leaves and turns them a glittering silver. A cricket sizzles its way through the long grass. The stream murmurs at the bottom of the hill—that stream where you and I lingered on a golden afternoon in May.

I sit here and think of you and try to see your slim brown hand resting against this rock, feeling its warmth. I am aware again of the texture of your skin, the coolness of your feet, the sharp tingle of your fingertips. And in the pastures of my mind I run my hand over your quivering mouth and crush your tender breasts. Remembered passion grows sweeter with the passing of time.

You will not be thinking of me now, as you sit in your home in the city, cooking or sewing or trying to study for examinations. There will be men and women and children circling about you, in that crowded house of your grandmother's, and you will not be able to think of me for

46

more than a moment or two. But I know you do think of me sometimes, in some private moment which cuts you off from the crowd. You will remember how I wondered what it is all about, this loving, and why it should cause such an upheaval. You are still a child, Sushila—and yet you found it so easy to quieten my impatient heart.

On the night you came to stay with us, the light from the street lamp shone through the branches of the peach tree and made leaf patterns on the walls. Through the glass panes of the front door I caught a glimpse of little Sunil's face, bright and questing, and then—a hand—a dark, long-fingered hand that could only have belonged to you.

It was almost a year since I had seen you, my dark and slender girl. And now you were in your sixteenth year. And Sunil was twelve; and your uncle, Dinesh, who lived with me, was twenty-three. And I was almost thirty—a fearful and wonderful age, when life becomes dangerous for dreamers.

I remember that when I left Delhi last year, you cried. At first I thought it was because I was going away. Then I realized that it was because you could not go anywhere yourself. Did you envy my freedom—the freedom to live in a poverty of my own choosing, the freedom of the writer? Sunil, to my surprise, did not show much emotion at my going away. This hurt me a little, because during that year he had been particularly close to me, and I felt for him a very special love. But separations cannot be of any significance to small boys of twelve who live for today, tomorrow, and—if they are very serious—the day after.

Before I went away with Dinesh, you made us garlands of marigolds. They were orange and gold, fresh and clean and kissed by the sun. You garlanded me as I sat talking to Sunil. I remember you both as you both looked that day—Sunil's smile dimpling his cheeks, while you gazed at me very seriously, your expression very tender. I loved you even then . . .

Our first picnic.

The path to the little stream took us through the oak forest, where the flashy blue magpies played follow-my-leader with their harsh, creaky calls. Skirting an open ridge (the place where I now sit and write), the path dipped through oak, rhododendron and maple, until it reached a little knoll above the stream. It was a spot unknown to the tourists and summer visitors. Sometimes a milkman or woodcutter crossed the stream on the way to town or village but no one lived beside it. Wild roses grew on the banks.

I do not remember much of that picnic. There was a lot of dull conversation with our neighbours, the Kapoors, who had come along too. You and Sunil were rather bored. Dinesh looked preoccupied. He was fed up with college. He wanted to start earning a living: wanted to paint. His restlessness often made him moody, irritable.

Near the knoll the stream was too shallow for bathing, but I told Sunil about a cave and a pool further downstream and promised that we would visit the pool another day.

That same night, after dinner, we took a walk along the dark road that goes past the house and leads to the burning ghat. Sunil, who had already sensed the intimacy between us, took my hand and put it in yours. An odd, touching little gesture!

'Tell us a story,' you said.

'Yes, tell us,' said Sunil.

I told you the story of the pure in heart. A shepherd boy found a snake in the forest and the snake told the boy that it was really a princess who had been bewitched and turned into a snake, and that it could only recover its human form if someone who was truly pure in heart gave it three kisses on the mouth. The boy put his lips to the

*Ruskin Bond*

mouth of the snake and kissed it thrice. And the snake was transformed into a beautiful princess. But the boy lay cold and dead.

'You always tell sad stories,' complained Sunil.

'I like sad stories,' you said. 'Tell us another.'

'Tomorrow night. I'm sleepy.'

We were woken in the night by a strong wind which went whistling round the old house and came rushing down the chimney, humming and hawing and finally choking itself.

Sunil woke up and cried out, 'What's that noise, Uncle?'

'Only the wind,' I said.

'Not a ghost?'

'Well, perhaps the wind is made up of ghosts. Perhaps this wind contains the ghosts of all the people who have lived and died in this old house and want to come in again from the cold.'

You told me about a boy who had been fond of you in Delhi. Apparently he had visited the house on a few occasions, and had sometimes met you on the street while you were on your way home from school. At first, he had been fond of another girl but later he switched his affections to you. When you told me that he had written to you recently, and that before coming up you had replied to his letter, I was consumed by jealousy—an emotion which I thought I had grown out of long ago. It did not help to be told that you were not serious about the boy, that you were sorry for him because he had already been disappointed in love.

'If you feel sorry for everyone who has been disappointed in love,' I said, 'you will soon be receiving the affections of every young man over ten.'

'Let them give me their affections,' you said, 'and I will give them my chappal over their heads.'

'But spare my head,' I said.

'Have *you* been in love before?'

'Many times. But this is the first time.'

'And who is your love?'

'Haven't you guessed?'

Sunil, who was following our conversation with deep interest, seemed to revel in the situation. Probably he fancied himself playing the part of Cupid, or Kamadeva, and delighted in watching the arrows of love strike home. No doubt I made it more enjoyable for him. Because I could not hide my feelings. Soon Dinesh would know, too—and then?

A year ago my feelings about you were almost paternal! Or so I thought . . . But you are no longer a child and I am a little older too. For when, the night after the picnic, you took my hand and held it against your soft warm cheek, it was the first time that a girl had responded to me so readily, so tenderly. Perhaps it was just innocence but that one action of yours, that acceptance of me, immediately devastated my heart.

Gently, fervently, I kissed your eyes and forehead, your small round mouth, and the lobes of your ears, and your long smooth throat; and I whispered, 'Sushila, I love you, I love you, I love you,' in the same way that millions and millions of love-smitten young men have whispered since time immemorial. What else can one say? I love you, I love you. There is nothing simpler; nothing that can be made to mean any more than that. And what else did I say? That I would look after you and work for you and make you happy; and that too had been said before, and I was in no way different from anyone. I was a man and yet I was a boy again.

We visited the stream again, a day or two later, early in the morning. Using the rocks as stepping stones, we wandered downstream for about a furlong until we reached a pool and a small waterfall and a cool dark cave. The rocks were mostly grey but some were yellow with age and some were cushioned with moss. A forktail stood on a boulder in the middle of the stream, uttering its low pleasant call. Water came dripping down from the sides of the cave, while sunlight filtered through a crevice in the rock ceiling, dappling your face. A spray of water was caught by a shaft of sunlight and at intervals it reflected the colours of the rainbow.

'It is a beautiful place,' you said.

'Come, then,' I said, 'let us bathe.'

Sunil and I removed our clothes and jumped into the pool while you sat down in the shade of a walnut tree and watched us disport ourselves in the water. Like a frog, Sunil leapt and twisted about in the clear, icy water; his eyes shone, his teeth glistened white, his body glowed with sunshine, youth, and the jewels made by drops of water glistening in the sun.

Then we stretched ourselves out beside you and allowed the sun to sink deep into our bodies.

Your feet, laved with dew, stood firm on the quickening grass. There was a butterfly between us: its wings red and gold and heavy with dew. It could not move because of the weight of moisture. And as your foot came nearer and I saw that you would crush it, I said, 'Wait. Don't crush the butterfly, Sushila. It has only a few days in the sun and we have many.'

'And if I spare it,' you said, laughing, 'what will you do for me, what will you pay?'

'Why, anything you say.'

'And will you kiss my foot?'

'Both feet,' I said and did so willingly. For they were no less than the wings of butterflies.

Later, when you ventured near the water, I dragged you in with me. You cried out, not in alarm but with the shock of the cold water, and then, wrenching yourself from my arms, clambered on to the rocks, your thin dress clinging to your thighs, your feet making long patterns on the smooth stone.

Though we tired ourselves out that day, we did not sleep at night. We lay together, you and Sunil on either side of me. Your head rested on my shoulders, your hair lay pressed against my cheek. Sunil had curled himself up into a ball but he was far from being asleep. He took my hand, and he took yours, and he placed them together. And I kissed the tender inside of your hand.

I whispered to you, 'Sushila, there has never been anyone I've loved so much. I've been waiting all these years to find you. For a long time I did not even like women. But you are so different. You care for me, don't you?'

You nodded in the darkness. I could see the outline of your face in the faint moonlight that filtered through the skylight. You never replied directly to a question. I suppose that was a feminine quality; coyness, perhaps.

'Do you love me, Sushila?'

No answer.

'Not now. When you are a little older. In a year or two.'

Did she nod in the darkness or did I imagine it?

'I know it's too early,' I continued. 'You are still too young. You are still at school. But already you are much wiser than me. I am finding it too difficult to control myself, but I will, since you wish it so. I'm very impatient, I know that, but I'll wait for as long as you make me—two or three or a hundred years. Yes, Sushila, a hundred years!'

Ah, what a pretty speech I made! Romeo could have used some of it; Majnu, too.

And your answer? Just a nod, a little pressure on my hand.

*Ruskin Bond*

I took your fingers and kissed them one by one. Long fingers, as long as mine.

After some time I became aware of Sunil nudging me.

'You are not talking to me,' he complained. 'You are only talking to her. You only love her.'

'I'm terribly sorry. I love you too, Sunil.'

Content with this assurance, he fell asleep; but towards morning, thinking himself in the middle of the bed, he rolled over and landed with a thump on the floor. He didn't know how it had happened and accused me of pushing him out.

'I know you don't want me in the bed,' he said.

It was a good thing Dinesh, in the next room, didn't wake up.

*

'Have you done any work this week?' asked Dinesh with a look of reproach.

'Not much,' I said.

'You are hardly ever in the house. You are never at your desk. Something seems to have happened to you.'

'I have given myself a holiday, that's all. Can't writers take holidays too?'

'No. You have said so yourself. And anyway, you seem to have taken a permanent holiday.'

'Have you finished that painting of the Tibetan woman?' I asked, trying to change the subject.

'That's the third time you've asked me that question, even though you saw the completed painting a week ago. You're getting very absent-minded.'

There was a letter from your old boyfriend; I mean your young boyfriend. It was addressed to Sunil, but I recognized the sender's name and knew it was really for you.

I assumed a look of calm detachment and handed the letter to you. But both you and Sunil sensed my dismay. At first you teased me and showed me the boy's photograph, which had been enclosed (he was certainly good-looking in a flashy way); then, finding that I became gloomier every minute, you tried to make amends, assuring me that the correspondence was one-sided and that you no longer replied to his letters.

And that night, to show me that you really cared, you gave me your hand as soon as the lights were out. Sunil was fast asleep.

We sat together at the foot of your bed. I kept my arm about you, while you rested your head against my chest. Your feet lay in repose upon mine. I kept kissing you. And when we lay down together, I loosened your blouse and kissed your small firm breasts, and put my lips to your nipples and felt them grow hard against my mouth.

The shy responsiveness of your kisses soon turned to passion. You clung to me. We had forgotten time and place and circumstance. The light of your eyes had been drowned in that lost look of a woman who desires. For a space we both struggled against desire. Suddenly I had become afraid of myself—afraid for you. I tried to free myself from your clasping arms. But you cried in a low voice, 'Love me! Love me! I want you to love me.'

Another night you fell asleep with your face in the crook of my arm, and I lay awake a long time, conscious of your breathing, of the touch of your hair on my cheek, of the soft warm soles of your feet, of your slim waist and legs.

And in the morning, when the sunshine filled the room, I watched you while you slept—your slim body in repose, your face tranquil, your thin dark hands like sleeping butterflies and then, when you woke, the beautiful untidiness of your hair and the drowsiness in your eyes. You lay folded up like a kitten, your limbs as untouched by self-consciousness as the limbs of a young and growing tree. And during the warmth of the day a bead of sweat rested on your brow like a small pearl.

I tried to remember what you looked like as a child. Even then, I had always been aware of your presence. You must have been nine or ten when I first saw you—thin, dark, plain-faced, always wearing the faded green skirt that was your school uniform. You went about barefoot. Once, when the monsoon arrived, you ran out into the rain with the other children, naked, exulting in the swish of the cool rain. I remembered your beautiful straight legs and thighs, your swift smile, your dark eyes. You say you do not remember playing naked in the rain but that is because you did not see yourself.

I did not notice you growing. Your face did not change very much. You must have been thirteen when you gave up skirts and started wearing the salwar kameez. You had few clothes but the plainness of your dress only seemed to bring out your own radiance. And as you grew older, your eyes became more expressive, your hair longer and glossier, your gestures more graceful. And then, when you came to me in the hills, I found that you had been transformed into a fairy princess of devastating charm.

We were idling away the afternoon on our beds and you were reclining in my arms when Dinesh came in unexpectedly. He said nothing, merely passed through the room and entered his studio. Sunil got a fright and you were momentarily confused. Then you said, 'He knows already,' and I said, 'Yes, he must know.'

Later I spoke to Dinesh. I told him that I wanted to marry; that I knew I would have to wait until you were older and had finished school—probably two or three years—and that I was prepared to wait although I knew it would be a long and difficult business. I asked him to help me.

He was upset at first, probably because he felt I had been deceptive (which was true), and also because of his own responsibility in the matter. You were his niece and I had made love to you while he had been preoccupied with other things. But after a little while when he saw that I was sincere and rather confused he relented.

'It has happened too soon,' he said. 'She is too young for all this. Have you told her that you love her?'

'Of course. Many times.'

'You're a fool, then. Have you told her that you want to marry her?'

'Yes.'

'Fool again. That's not the way it is done. Haven't you lived in India long enough to know that?'

'But I love her.'

'Does she love you?'

'I think so.'

'You think so. Desire isn't love, you must know that. Still, I suppose she does love you, otherwise she would not be holding hands with you all day. But you are quite mad, falling in love with a girl half your age.'

'Well, I'm not exactly an old man. I'm thirty.'

'And she's a schoolgirl.'

'She isn't a girl any more, she's too responsive.'

'Oh, you've found that out, have you?'

'Well . . .' I said, covered in confusion. 'Well, she has shown that she cares a little. You know that it's years since I took any interest in a girl. You called it unnatural on my part, remember? Well, they simply did not exist for me, that's true.'

'Delayed adolescence,' muttered Dinesh.

'But Sushila is different. She puts me at ease. She doesn't

*Ruskin Bond*

turn away from me. I love her and I want to look after her. I can only do that by marrying her.'

'All right, but take it easy. Don't get carried away. And don't, for God's sake, give her a baby. Not while she's still at school! I will do what I can to help you. But you will have to be patient. And no one else must know of this or I will be blamed for everything. As it is Sunil knows too much, and he's too small to know so much.'

'Oh, he won't tell anyone.'

'I wish you had fallen in love with her two years from now. You will have to wait that long, anyway. Getting married isn't a simple matter. People will wonder why we are in such a hurry, marrying her off as soon as she leaves school. They'll think the worst!'

'Well, people do marry for love you know, even in India. It's happening all the time.'

'But it doesn't happen in our family. You know how orthodox most of them are. They wouldn't appreciate your outlook. You may marry Sushila for love but it will have to look like an arranged marriage!'

Little things went wrong that evening.

First, a youth on the road passed a remark which you resented; and you, most unladylike, but most Punjabi-like, picked up a stone and threw it at him. It struck him on the leg. He was too surprised to say anything and limped off. I remonstrated with you, told you that throwing stones at people often resulted in a fight, then realized that you had probably wanted to see me fighting on your behalf.

Later you were annoyed because I said you were a little absent-minded. Then Sunil sulked because I spoke roughly to him (I can't remember why), and refused to talk to me for three hours, which was a record. I kept apologizing but neither of you would listen. It was all part of a game. When I gave up trying and turned instead to my typewriter and my unfinished story, you came and sat beside me and started playing with my hair. You were jealous of my story, of the fact that it was possible for me to withdraw into my work. And I reflected that a woman had to be jealous of something. If there wasn't another woman, then it was a man's work, or his hobby, or his best friend, or his favourite sweater, or his pet mongoose that made her resentful. There is a story in Kipling about a woman who grew insanely jealous of a horse's saddle because her husband spent an hour every day polishing it with great care and loving kindness.

Would it be like that in marriage, I wondered—an eternal triangle: you, me and the typewriter?

But there were only a few days left before you returned to the plains, so I gladly pushed away the typewriter and took you in my arms instead. After all, once you had gone away, it would be a long, long time before I could hold you in my arms again. I might visit you in Delhi but we would not be able to enjoy the same freedom and intimacy. And while I savoured the salt kiss of your lips, I wondered how long I would have to wait until I could really call you my own.

Dinesh was at college and Sunil had gone roller skating and we were alone all morning. At first you avoided me, so I picked up a book and pretended to read. But barely five minutes had passed before you stole up from behind and snapped the book shut.

'It is a warm day,' you said. 'Let us go down to the stream.'

Alone together for the first time, we took the steep path down to the stream, and there, hand in hand, scrambled over the rocks until we reached the pool and the waterfall.

'I will bathe today,' you said; and in a few moments you stood beside me, naked, caressed by sunlight and a soft

*Ruskin Bond*

breeze coming down the valley. I put my hand out to share in the sun's caress, but you darted away, laughing, and ran to the waterfall as though you would hide behind a curtain of gushing water. I was soon beside you. I took you in my arms and kissed you, while the water crashed down upon our heads. Who yielded—you or I? All I remember is that you had entwined yourself about me like a clinging vine, and that a little later we lay together on the grass, on bruised and broken clover, while a whistling thrush released its deep sweet secret on the trembling air.

Blackbird on the wing, bird of the forest shadows, black rose in the long ago of summer, this was your song. It isn't time that's passing by, it is you and I.

It was your last night under my roof. We were not alone but when I woke in the middle of the night and stretched my hand out, across the space between our beds, you took my hand, for you were awake too. Then I pressed the ends of your fingers, one by one, as I had done so often before, and you dug your nails into my flesh. And our hands made love, much as our bodies might have done. They clung together, warmed and caressed each other, each finger taking on an identity of its own and seeking its opposite. Sometimes the tips of our fingers merely brushed against each other, teasingly, and sometimes our palms met with a rush, would tremble and embrace, separate, and then passionately seek each other out. And when sleep finally overcame you, your hand fell listlessly between our beds, touching the ground. And I lifted it up, and after putting it once to my lips, returned it gently to your softly rising bosom.

And so you went away, all three of you, and I was left alone with the brooding mountain. If I could not pass a few weeks without you how was I to pass a year, two years? This was the question I kept asking myself. Would

I have to leave the hills and take a flat in Delhi? And what use would it be—looking at you and speaking to you but never able to touch you? Not to be able to touch that which I had already possessed would have been the subtlest form of torture.

The house was empty but I kept finding little things to remind me that you had been there—a handkerchief, a bangle, a length of ribbon—and these remnants made me feel as though you had gone for ever. No sound at night, except the rats scurrying about on the rafters.

The rain had brought out the ferns, which were springing up from tree and rock. The murmur of the stream had become an angry rumble. The honeysuckle creeper winding over the front windows was thick with scented blossom. I wish it had flowered a little earlier, before you left. Then you could have put the flowers in your hair.

At night I drank brandy, wrote listlessly, listened to the wind in the chimney, and read poetry in bed. There was no one to tell stories to and no hand to hold.

I kept remembering little things—the soft hair hiding your ears, the movement of your hands, the cool touch of your feet, the tender look in your eyes and the sudden stab of mischief that sometimes replaced it.

Mrs Kapoor remarked on the softness of your expression. I was glad that someone had noticed it. In my diary I wrote: 'I have looked at Sushila so often and so much that perhaps I have overlooked her most compelling qualities— her kindness (or is it just her easy-goingness?), her refusal to hurt anyone's feelings (or is it just her indifference to everything?), her wide tolerance (or is it just her laziness?) . . . Oh, how absolutely ignorant I am of women!'

Well, there was a letter from Dinesh and it held out a lifeline, one that I knew I must seize without any hesitation. He said he might be joining an art school in Delhi and asked me if I would like to return to Delhi and share a flat with him. I had always dreaded the possibility of leaving the hills and living again in a city as depressing as Delhi but love, I considered, ought to make any place habitable . . .

And then I was on a bus on the road to Delhi.

The first monsoon showers had freshened the fields and everything looked much greener than usual. The maize was just shooting up and the mangoes were ripening fast. Near the larger villages, camels and bullock carts cluttered up the road, and the driver cursed, banging his fist on the horn.

Passing through small towns, the bus driver had to contend with cycle rickshaws, tonga ponies, trucks, pedestrians, and other buses. Coming down from the hills for the first time in over a year, I found the noise, chaos, dust and dirt a little unsettling.

As my taxi drew up at the gate of Dinesh's home, Sunil saw me and came running to open the car door. Other children were soon swarming around me. Then I saw you standing near the front door. You raised your hand to your forehead in a typical Muslim form of greeting—a gesture you had picked up, I suppose, from a film.

For two days Dinesh and I went house hunting, for I had decided to take a flat if it was at all practicable. Either it was very hot, and we were sweating, or it was raining and we were drenched. (It is difficult to find a flat in Delhi, even if one is in a position to pay an exorbitant rent, which I was not. It is especially difficult for bachelors. No one trusts bachelors, especially if there are grown-up daughters in the house. Is this because bachelors are wolves or because girls are so easily seduced these days?)

Finally, after several refusals, we were offered a flat in one of those new colonies that sprout like mushrooms around the capital. The rent was two hundred rupees a month and although I knew I couldn't really afford so much, I was so sick of refusals and already so disheartened and depressed that I took the place and made out a cheque to the landlord, an elderly gentleman with his daughters all safely married in other parts of the country.

There was no furniture in the flat except for a couple of beds, but we decided we would fill the place up gradually. Everyone at Dinesh's home—brothers, sister-in-law, aunts, nephews and nieces—helped us to move in. Sunil and his younger brother were the first arrivals. Later the other children, some ten of them, arrived. You, Sushila, came only in the afternoon, but I had gone out for something and only saw you when I returned at tea time. You were sitting on the first-floor balcony and smiled down at me as I walked up the road.

I think you were pleased with the flat; or at any rate, with my courage in taking one. I took you up to the roof, and there, in a corner under the stairs, kissed you very quickly. It had to be quick, because the other children were close on our heels. There wouldn't be much opportunity for kissing you again. The mountains were far and in a place like Delhi, and with a family like yours, private moments would be few and far between.

Hours later when I sat alone on one of the beds, Sunil came to me, looking rather upset. He must have had a quarrel with you.

'I want to tell you something,' he said.

'Is anything wrong?'

To my amazement he burst into tears.

'Now you must not love me any more,' he said.

'Why not?'

'Because you are going to marry Sushila, and if you love me too much it will not be good for you.'

I could think of nothing to say. It was all too funny and all too sad.

But a little later he was in high spirits, having apparently forgotten the reasons for his earlier dejection. His need for affection stemmed perhaps from his father's long and unnecessary absence from the country.

Dinesh and I had no sleep during our first night in the new flat. We were near the main road and traffic roared past all night. I thought of the hills, so silent that the call of a nightjar startled one in the stillness of the night.

I was out most of the next day and when I got back in the evening it was to find that Dinesh had had a rumpus with the landlord. Apparently the landlord had really wanted bachelors, and couldn't understand or appreciate a large number of children moving in and out of the house all day.

'I thought landlords preferred having families,' I said.

'He wants to know how a bachelor came to have such a large family!'

'Didn't you tell him that the children were only temporary, and wouldn't be living here?'

'I did, but he doesn't believe me.'

'Well, anyway, we're not going to stop the children from coming to see us,' I said indignantly. (No children, no Sushila!) 'If he doesn't see reason, he can have his flat back.'

'Did he cash my cheque?'

'No, he's given it back.'

'That means he really wants us out. To hell with his flat! It's too noisy here anyway. Let's go back to your place.'

We packed our bedding, trunks and kitchen utensils once more; hired a bullock cart and arrived at Dinesh's home (three miles distant) late at night, hungry and upset.

Everything seemed to be going wrong.

Living in the same house as you, but unable to have any real contact with you (except for the odd, rare moment when we were left alone in the same room and were able to exchange a word or a glance) was an exquisite form of self-inflicted torture: self-inflicted, because no one was forcing me to stay in Delhi. Sometimes you had to avoid me and I could not stand that. Only Dinesh (and, of course, Sunil and some of the children) knew anything about the affair—adults are much slower than children at sensing the truth—and it was still too soon to reveal the true state of affairs and my own feelings to anyone else in the family. If I came out with the declaration that I was in love with you, it would immediately become obvious that something had happened during your holiday in the hill station. It would be said that I had taken advantage of the situation (which I had), and that I had seduced you—even though I was beginning to wonder if it was you who had seduced me! And if a marriage was suddenly arranged, people would say: 'It's been arranged so quickly. And she's so young. He must have got her into trouble.' Even though there were no signs of your having got into that sort of trouble.

And yet I could not help hoping that you would become my wife sooner than could be foreseen. I wanted to look after you. I did not want others to be doing it for me. Was that very selfish? Or was it a true state of being in love?

There were times—times when you kept at a distance and did not even look at me—when I grew desperate. I knew you could not show your familiarity with me in front of others and yet, knowing this, I still tried to catch your eye, to sit near you, to touch you fleetingly. I could not hold myself back. I became morose, I wallowed in self-pity. And self-pity, I realized, is a sign of failure, especially of failure in love.

*Ruskin Bond*

It was time to return to the hills.

Sushila, when I got up in the morning to leave, you were still asleep and I did not wake you. I watched you stretched out on your bed, your dark face tranquil and untouched by care, your black hair spread over the white pillow, your long thin hands and feet in repose. You were so beautiful when you were asleep.

And as I watched, I felt a tightening around my heart, a sudden panic that I might somehow lose you.

The others were up and there was no time to steal a kiss. A taxi was at the gate. A baby was bawling. Your grandmother was giving me advice. The taxi driver kept blowing his horn.

Goodbye, Sushila!

We were in the middle of the rains. There was a constant drip and drizzle and drumming on the corrugated tin roof. The walls were damp and there was mildew on my books and even on the pickle that Dinesh had made.

Everything was green, the foliage almost tropical, especially near the stream. Great stag ferns grew from the trunks of tree fresh moss covered the rocks, and the maidenhair fern was at its loveliest. The water was a torrent, rushing through the ravine and taking with it bushes and small trees. I could not remain out for long, for at any moment it might start raining. And there were also the leeches who lost no time in fastening themselves on to my legs and feasting on my blood.

Once, standing on some rocks, I saw a slim brown snake swimming with the current. It looked beautiful and lonely.

I dreamt a dream, very disturbing dream, which troubled me for days.

In the dream, Sunil suggested that we go down to the stream.

We put some bread and butter into an airbag, along with

a long bread knife, and set off down the hill. Sushila was barefoot, wearing the old cotton tunic which she had worn as a child, Sunil had on a bright yellow T-shirt and black jeans. He looked very dashing. As we took the forest path down to the stream, we saw two young men following us. One of them, a dark, slim youth, seemed familiar. I said, 'Isn't that Sushila's boyfriend?' But they denied it. The other youth wasn't anyone I knew.

When we reached the stream, Sunil and I plunged into the pool, while Sushila sat on the rock just above us. We had been bathing for a few minutes when the two young men came down the slope and began fondling Sushila. She did not resist but Sunil climbed out of the pool and began scrambling up the slope. One of the youths, the less familiar one, had a long knife in his hand. Sunil picked up a stone and flung it at the youth, striking him on the shoulder. I rushed up and grabbed the hand that held the knife. The youth kicked me on the shins and thrust me away and I fell beneath him. The arm with the knife was raised over me, but I still held the wrist. And then I saw Sushila behind him, her face framed by a passing cloud. She had the bread knife in her hand, and her arm swung up and down, and the knife cut through my adversary's neck as though it were passing through a ripe melon.

I scrambled to my feet to find Sushila gazing at the headless corpse with the detachment and mild curiosity of a child who has just removed the wings from a butterfly.

The other youth, who looked like Sushila's boyfriend, began running away. He was chased by the three of us. When he slipped and fell, I found myself beside him, the blade of the knife poised beneath his left shoulder blade. I couldn't push the knife in. Then Sunil put his hand over mine and the blade slipped smoothly into the flesh.

At all times of the day and night I could hear the

murmur of the stream at the bottom of the hill. Even if I didn't listen, the sound was there. I had grown used to it. But whenever I went away, I was conscious of something missing and I was lonely without the sound of running water.

I remained alone for two months and then I had to see you again, Sushila. I could not bear the long-drawn-out uncertainty of the situation. I wanted to do something that would bring everything nearer to a conclusion. Merely to stand by and wait was intolerable. Nor could I bear the secrecy to which Dinesh had sworn me. Someone else would have to know about my intentions—someone would have to help. I needed another ally to sustain my hopes; only then would I find the waiting easier.

You had not been keeping well and looked thin, but you were as cheerful, as serene as ever.

When I took you to the pictures with Sunil, you wore a sleeveless kameez made of purple silk. It set off your dark beauty very well. Your face was soft and shy and your smile hadn't changed. I could not keep my eyes off you.

Returning home in the taxi, I held your hand all the way.

Sunil (in Punjabi): 'Will you give your children English or Hindi names?'

Me: 'Hindustani names.'

Sunil (in Punjabi): 'Ah, that is the right answer, Uncle!'

And first I went to your mother.

She was a tiny woman and looked very delicate. But she'd had six children—a seventh was on the way—and they had all come into the world without much difficulty and were the healthiest in the entire joint family.

She was on her way to see relatives in another part of the city and I accompanied her part of the way. As she was pregnant, she was offered a seat in the crowded bus. I managed to squeeze in beside her. She had always shown a liking for me and I did not find it difficult to come to the point.

'At what age would you like Sushila to get married?' I asked casually, with almost paternal interest.

'We'll worry about that when the time comes. She has still to finish school. And if she keeps failing her exams, she will never finish school.'

I took a deep breath and made the plunge.

'When the time comes,' I said, 'when the time comes, I would like to marry her.' And without waiting to see what her reaction would be, I continued: 'I know I must wait, a year or two, even longer. But I am telling you this, so that it will be in your mind. You are her mother and so I want you to be the first to know.' (Liar that I was! She was about the fifth to know. But what I really wanted to say was, 'Please don't be looking for any other husband for her just yet.')

She didn't show much surprise. She was a placid woman. But she said, rather sadly, 'It's all right but I don't have much say in the family. I do not have any money, you see. It depends on the others, especially her grandmother.'

'I'll speak to them when the time comes. Don't worry about that. And you don't have to worry about money or anything—what I mean is, I don't believe in dowries—I mean, you don't have to give me a Godrej cupboard and a sofa set and that sort of thing. All I want is Sushila . . .'

'She is still very young.'

But she was pleased—pleased that her flesh and blood, her own daughter, could mean so much to a man.

'Don't tell anyone else just now,' I said.

'I won't tell anyone,' she said with a smile.

So now the secret—if it could be called that—was shared by at least five people.

The bus crawled on through the busy streets and we sat in silence, surrounded by a press of people but isolated in the intimacy of our conversation.

I warmed towards her—towards that simple, straightforward, uneducated woman (she had never been to school, could not read or write), who might still have been young and pretty had her circumstances been different. I asked her when the baby was due.

'In two months,' she said. She laughed. Evidently she found it unusual and rather amusing for a young man to ask her such a question.

'I'm sure it will be a fine baby,' I said. And I thought: That makes six brothers-in-law!

I did not think I would get a chance to speak to your Uncle Ravi (Dinesh's elder brother) before I left. But on my last evening in Delhi, I found myself alone with him on the Karol Bagh road. At first we spoke of his own plans for marriage, and, to please him, I said the girl he'd chosen was both beautiful and intelligent.

He warmed towards me.

Clearing my throat, I went on. 'Ravi, you are five years younger than me and you are about to get married.'

'Yes, and it's time you thought of doing the same thing.'

'Well, I've never thought seriously about it before—I'd always scorned the institution of marriage—but now I've changed my mind. Do you know whom I'd like to marry?'

To my surprise Ravi unhesitatingly took the name of Asha, a distant cousin I'd met only once. She came from Ferozepur, and her hips were so large that from a distance she looked like an oversized pear.

'No, no,' I said. 'Asha is a lovely girl but I wasn't thinking of her. I would like to marry a girl like Sushila. To be frank, Ravi, I would like to marry Sushila.'

There was a long silence and I feared the worst. The

noise of cars, scooters and buses seemed to recede into the distance and Ravi and I were alone together in a vacuum of silence.

So that the awkwardness would not last too long, I stumbled on with what I had to say. 'I know she's young and that I will have to wait for some time.' (Familiar words!) 'But if you approve, and the family approves, and Sushila approves, well then, there's nothing I'd like better than to marry her.'

Ravi pondered, scratched himself, and then, to my delight, said: 'Why not? It's a fine idea.'

The traffic sounds returned to the street, and I felt as though I could set fire to a bus or do something equally in keeping with my high spirits.

'It would bring you even closer to us,' said Ravi. 'We would like to have you in our family. At least I would like it.'

'That makes all the difference,' I said. 'I will do my best for her, Ravi. I'll do everything to make her happy.'

'She is very simple and unspoilt.'

'I know. That's why I care so much for her.'

'I will do what I can to help you. She should finish school by the time she is seventeen. It does not matter if you are older. Twelve years difference in age is not uncommon. So don't worry. Be patient and all will be arranged.'

And so I had three strong allies—Dinesh, Ravi and your mother. Only your grandmother remained, and I dared not approach her on my own. She was the most difficult hurdle because she was the head of the family and she was autocratic and often unpredictable. She was not on good terms with your mother and for that very reason I feared that she might oppose my proposal. I had no idea how much she valued Ravi's and Dinesh's judgement. All I knew was that they bowed to all her decisions.

How impossible it was for you to shed the burden of your relatives! Individually, you got on quite well with all of them; but because they could not live without bickering among themselves, you were just a pawn in the great Joint Family Game.

You put my hand to your cheek and to your breast. I kissed your closed eyes and took your face in my hands, and touched your lips with mine; a phantom kiss in the darkness of a veranda. And then, intoxicated, I stumbled into the road and walked the streets all night.

I was sitting on the rocks above the oak forest when I saw a young man walking towards me down the steep path. From his careful manner of walking, and light clothing, I could tell that he was a stranger, one who was not used to the hills. He was about my height, slim, rather long in the face; good looking in a delicate sort of way. When he came nearer, I recognized him as the young man in the photograph, the youth of my dream—your late admirer! I wasn't too surprised to see him. Somehow, I had always felt that we would meet one day.

I remembered his name and said, 'How are you, Pramod?'

He became rather confused. His eyes were already clouded with doubt and unhappiness; but he did not appear to be an aggressive person.

'How did you know my name?' he asked.

'How did you know where to find me?' I countered.

'Your neighbours, the Kapoors, told me. I could not wait for you to return to the house. I have to go down again tonight.'

'Well then, would you like to walk home with me, or would you prefer to sit here and talk? I know who you are but I've no idea why you've come to see me.'

'It's all right here,' he said, spreading his handkerchief on the grass before sitting down on it. 'How did you know my name?'

I stared at him for a few moments and got the impression that he was a vulnerable person—perhaps more vulnerable than myself. My only advantage was that I was older and therefore better able to conceal my real feelings.

'Sushila told me,' I said.

'Oh. I did not think you would know.'

I was a little puzzled but said, 'I knew about you, of course. And you must have known that or you would hardly have come here to see me.'

'You knew about Sushila and me?' he asked, looking even more confused.

'Well, I know that you are supposed to be in love with her.'

He smote himself on the forehead. 'My God! Do the others know, too?'

'I don't think so.' I deliberately avoided mention of Sunil.

In his distraction he started plucking at tufts of grass. 'Did she tell you?' he asked.

'Yes.'

'Girls can't keep secrets. But in a way I'm glad she told you. Now I don't have to explain everything. You see, I came here for your help. I know you are not her real uncle but you are very close to her family. Last year in Delhi she often spoke about you. She said you were very kind.'

It then occurred to me that Pramod knew nothing about my relationship with you, other than that I was supposed to be the most benevolent of 'uncles'. He knew that you had spent your summer holidays with me—but so had Dinesh and Sunil. And now, aware that I was a close friend of the family, he had come to make an ally of me—in much the same way that I had gone about making allies!

'Have you seen Sushila recently?' I asked.

'Yes. Two days ago, in Delhi. But I had only a few

minutes alone with her. We could not talk much. You see, Uncle—you will not mind if I also call you uncle? I want to marry her but there is no one who can speak to her people on my behalf. My own parents are not alive. If I go straight to her family, most probably I will be thrown out of the house. So I want you to help me. I am not well off but I will soon have a job and then I can support her.'

'Did you tell her all this?'

'Yes.'

'And what did she say?'

'She told me to speak to you about it.'

Clever Sushila! Diabolical Sushila!

'To me?' I repeated.

'Yes, she said it would be better than talking to her parents.'

I couldn't help laughing. And a long-tailed blue magpie, disturbed by my laughter, set up a shrill creaking and chattering of its own.

'Don't laugh, I'm serious, Uncle,' said Pramod. He took me by the hand and looked at me appealingly.

'Well, it ought to be serious,' I said. 'How old are you, Pramod?'

'Twenty-three.'

'Only seven years younger than me. So please don't call me uncle. It makes me feel prehistoric. Use my first name, if you like. And when do you hope to marry Sushila?'

'As soon as possible. I know she is still very young for me.'

'Not at all,' I said. 'Young girls are marrying middle-aged men every day! And you're still quite young yourself. But she can't get married as yet, Pramod, I know that for a certainty.'

'That's what I feared. She will have to finish school, I suppose.'

'That's right. But tell me something. It's obvious that you are in love with her and I don't blame you for it. Sushila is the kind of girl we all fall in love with! But do you know if she loves you? Did she say she would like to marry you?'

'She did not say—I do not know . . .' There was a haunted, hurt look in his eyes and my heart went out to him. 'But I love her—isn't that enough?'

'It could be enough—provided she doesn't love someone else.'

'Does she, Uncle?'

'To be frank, I don't know.'

He brightened up at that. 'She likes me,' he said. 'I know that much.'

'Well, I like you too, but that doesn't mean I'd marry you.'

He was despondent again. 'I see what you mean . . . But what is love, how can I recognize it?'

And that was one question I couldn't answer. How do we recognize it?

I persuaded Pramod to stay the night. The sun had gone down and he was shivering. I made a fire, the first of the winter, using oak and thorn branches. Then I shared my brandy with him.

I did not feel any resentment against Pramod. Prior to meeting him, I had been jealous. And when I first saw him coming along the path, I remembered my dream, and thought, 'Perhaps I am going to kill him, after all. Or perhaps he's going to kill me.' But it had turned out differently. If dreams have any meaning at all, the meaning doesn't come within our limited comprehension.

I had visualized Pramod as being rather crude, selfish and irresponsible, an unattractive college student, the type who has never known or understood girls very well and looks on them as strange exotic creatures who are to be

74          *Ruskin Bond*

seized and plundered at the first opportunity. Such men do exist but Pramod was never one of them. He did not know much about women; neither did I. He was gentle, polite, unsure of himself. I wondered if I should tell him about my own feelings for you.

After a while he began to talk about himself and about you. He told me how he fell in love with you. At first he had been friendly with another girl, a class fellow of yours but a year or two older. You had carried messages to him on the girl's behalf. Then the girl had rejected him. He was terribly depressed and one evening he drank a lot of cheap liquor. Instead of falling dead, as he had been hoping, he lost his way and met you near your home. He was in need of sympathy and you gave him that. You let him hold your hand. He told you how hopeless he felt and you comforted him. And when he said the world was a cruel place, you consented. You agreed with him. What more can a man expect from a woman? Only fourteen at the time, you had no difficulty in comforting a man of twenty-two. No wonder he fell in love with you!

Afterwards you met occasionally on the road and spoke to each other. He visited the house once or twice, on some pretext or other. And when you came to the hills, he wrote to you.

That was all he had to tell me. That was all there was to tell. You had touched his heart once and touching it, had no difficulty in capturing it.

Next morning I took Pramod down to the stream. I wanted to tell him everything and somehow I could not do it in the house.

He was charmed by the place. The water flowed gently, its music subdued, soft chamber music after the monsoon orchestration. Cowbells tinkled on the hillside and an eagle soared high above.

'I did not think water could be so clear,' said Pramod. 'It is not muddy like the streams and rivers of the plains.'

'In the summer you can bathe here,' I said. 'There is a pool further downstream.'

He nodded thoughtfully. 'Did she come here too?'

'Yes, Sushila and Sunil and I . . . We came here on two or three occasions.' My voice trailed off and I glanced at Pramod standing at the edge of the water. He looked up at me and his eyes met mine.

'There is something I want to tell you,' I said.

He continued staring at me and a shadow seemed to pass across his face—a shadow of doubt, fear, death, eternity, was it one or all of these, or just a play of light and shade? But I remembered my dream and stepped back from him. For a moment both of us looked at each other with distrust and uncertainty. Then the fear passed. Whatever had happened between us, dream or reality, had happened in some other existence. Now he took my hand and held it, held it tight, as though seeking assurance, as though identifying himself with me.

'Let us sit down,' I said. 'There is something I must tell you.'

We sat down on the grass and when I looked up through the branches of the banj oak, everything seemed to have been tilted and held at an angle, and the sky shocked me with its blueness, and the leaves were no longer green but purple in the shadows of the ravine. They were your colour, Sushila. I remembered you wearing purple—dark smiling Sushila, thinking your own thoughts and refusing to share them with anyone.

'I love Sushila too,' I said.

'I know,' he said naïvely. 'That is why I came to you for help.'

'No, you don't know,' I said. 'When I say I love Sushila,

*Ruskin Bond*

I mean just that. I mean caring for her in the same way that you care for her. I mean I want to marry her.'

'You, Uncle?'

'Yes. Does it shock you very much?'

'No, no.' He turned his face away and stared at the worn face of an old grey rock and perhaps he drew some strength from its permanency. 'Why should you not love her? Perhaps, in my heart, I really knew it, but did not want to know—did not want to believe. Perhaps that is why I really came here—to find out. Something that Sunil said ... But why didn't you tell me before?'

'Because you were telling me!'

'Yes, I was too full of my own love to think that any other was possible. What do we do now? Do we both wait and then let her make her choice?'

'If you wish.'

'You have the advantage, Uncle. You have more to offer.'

'Do you mean more security or more love? Some women place more value on the former.'

'Not Sushila.'

'I mean you can offer her a more interesting life. You are a writer. Who knows, you may be famous one day.'

'You have your youth to offer, Pramod. I have only a few years of youth left to me—and two or three of them will pass in waiting.'

'Oh, no,' he said. 'You will always be young. If you have Sushila, you will always be young.'

Once again I heard the whistling thrush. Its song was a crescendo of sweet notes and variations that rang clearly across the ravine. I could not see the bird but its call emerged from the forest like some dark sweet secret and again it was saying, 'It isn't time that's passing by, my friend. It is you and I.'

Listen. Sushila, the worst has happened. Ravi has written to say that a marriage will not be possible—not now, not next year; never. Of course he makes a lot of excuses—that you must receive a complete college education ('higher studies'), that the difference in our age is too great, that you might change your mind after a year or two—but reading between the lines, I can guess that the real reason is your grandmother. She does not want it. Her word is law and no one, least of all Ravi, would dare oppose her.

But I do not mean to give in so easily. I will wait my chance. As long as I know that you are with me, I will wait my chance.

I wonder what the old lady objects to in me. Is it simply that she is conservative and tradition-bound? She has always shown a liking for me and I don't see why her liking should change because I want to marry her grandniece. Your mother has no objection. Perhaps that's why your grandmother objects.

Whatever the reason, I am coming down to Delhi to find out how things stand.

Of course the worst part is that Ravi has asked me—in the friendliest terms and in a most roundabout manner—not to come to the house for some time. He says this will give the affair a chance to cool off and die a natural (I would call it an unnatural) death. He assumes, of course, that I will accept the old lady's decision and simply forget all about you. Ravi is yet to fall in love.

Dinesh was in Lucknow. I could not visit the house. So I sat on a bench in the Talkatora Gardens and watched a group of children playing *gulli danda*. Then I recalled that Sunil's school got over at three o'clock and that if I hurried I would be able to meet him outside the St Columba's gate.

I reached the school on time. Boys were streaming out of the compound and as they were all wearing green uniforms—a young forest on the move—I gave up all hope of spotting Sunil. But he saw me first. He ran across the road, dodged a cyclist, evaded a bus and seized me about the waist.

'I'm so happy to see you, Uncle!'

'As I am to see you, Sunil.'

'You want to see Sushila?'

'Yes, but you too. I can't come to the house, Sunil. You probably know that. When do you have to be home?'

'About four o'clock. If I'm late, I'll say the bus was too crowded and I couldn't get in.'

'That gives us an hour or two. Let's go to the exhibition grounds. Would you like that?'

'All right, I haven't seen the exhibition yet.'

We took a scooter rickshaw to the exhibition grounds on Mathura Road. It was an industrial exhibition and there was little to interest either a schoolboy or a lovesick author. But a café was at hand, overlooking an artificial lake, and we sat in the sun consuming hot dogs and cold coffee.

'Sunil, will you help me?' I asked.

'Whatever you say, Uncle.'

'I don't suppose I can see Sushila this time. I don't want to hang about near the house or her school like a disreputable character. It's all right lurking outside a boys' school; but it wouldn't do to be hanging about the Kanyadevi Pathshala or wherever it is she's studying. It's possible the family will change their minds about us later. Anyway, what matters now is Sushila's attitude. Ask her this, Sunil. Ask her if she wants me to wait until she is eighteen. She will be free then to do what she wants, even to run away with me if necessary—that is, if she really wants to. I was ready to wait two years. I'm prepared to wait three. But it will help if I know she's waiting too. Will you ask her that, Sunil?'

'Yes, I'll ask her.'

'Ask her tonight. Then tomorrow we'll meet again outside your school.'

We met briefly the next day. There wasn't much time. Sunil had to be home early and I had to catch the night train out of Delhi. We stood in the generous shade of a peepul tree and I asked, 'What did she say?'

'She said to keep waiting.'

'All right, I'll wait.'

'But when she is eighteen, what if she changes her mind? You know what girls are like.'

'You're a cynical chap, Sunil.'

'What does that mean?'

'It means you know too much about life. But tell me—what makes you think she might change her mind?'

'Her boyfriend.'

'Pramod? She doesn't care for him, poor chap.'

'Not Pramod. Another one.'

'Another! You mean a new one?'

'New,' said Sunil. 'An officer in a bank. He's got a car.'

'Oh,' I said despondently. 'I can't compete with a car.'

'No,' said Sunil. 'Never mind, Uncle. You still have me for your friend. Have you forgotten that?'

I had almost forgotten but it was good to be reminded.

'It is time to go,' he said. 'I must catch the bus today. When will you come to Delhi again?'

'Next month. Next year. Who knows? But I'll come. Look after yourself, my friend.'

He ran off and jumped on to the footboard of a moving bus. He waved to me until the bus went round the bend in the road.

It was lonely under the peepul tree. It is said that only ghosts live in peepul trees. I do not blame them, for peepul trees are cool and shady and full of loneliness.

I may stop loving you, Sushila, but I will never stop loving the days I loved you.

# time stops at shamli

The Dehra Express usually drew into Shamli at about
five o'clock in the morning at which time the station
would be dimly lit and the jungle across the tracks would
just be visible in the faint light of dawn. Shamli is a small
station at the foot of the Siwalik hills and the Siwaliks lie
at the foot of the Himalayas, which in turn lie at the feet
of God.

The station, I remember, had only one platform, an office
for the stationmaster, and a waiting room. The platform
boasted a tea stall, a fruit vendor, and a few stray dogs. Not
much else was required because the train stopped at Shamli
for only five minutes before rushing on into the forests.

Why it stopped at Shamli, I never could tell. Nobody got
off the train and nobody got on. There were never any
coolies on the platform. But the train would stand there a
full five minutes and the guard would blow his whistle and
presently Shamli would be left behind and forgotten ...
until I passed that way again.

I was paying my relations in Saharanpur an annual visit
when the night train stopped at Shamli. I was thirty-six at
the time and still single.

On this particular journey, the train came into Shamli just as I awoke from a restless sleep. The third-class compartment was crowded beyond capacity and I had been sleeping in an upright position with my back to the lavatory door. Now someone was trying to get into the lavatory. He was obviously hard pressed for time.

'I'm sorry, brother,' I said, moving as much as I could to one side.

He stumbled into the closet without bothering to close the door.

'Where are we now?' I asked the man sitting beside me. He was smoking a strong aromatic beedi.

'Shamli station,' he said, rubbing the palm of a large calloused hand over the frosted glass of the window.

I let the window down and stuck my head out. There was a cool breeze blowing down the platform, a breeze that whispered of autumn in the hills. As usual there was no activity except for the fruit vendor walking up and down the length of the train with his basket of mangoes balanced on his head. At the tea stall, a kettle was steaming, but there was no one to mind it. I rested my forehead on the window ledge and let the breeze play on my temples. I had been feeling sick and giddy but there was a wild sweetness in the wind that I found soothing.

'Yes,' I said to myself, 'I wonder what happens in Shamli behind the station walls.'

My fellow passenger offered me a beedi. He was a farmer, I think, on his way to Dehra. He had a long, untidy, sad moustache.

We had been more than five minutes at the station. I looked up and down the platform, but nobody was getting on or off the train. Presently the guard came walking past our compartment.

'What's the delay?' I asked him.

'Some obstruction further down the line,' he said.

'Will we be here long?'

'I don't know what the trouble is. About half an hour at the least.'

My neighbour shrugged and throwing the remains of his beedi out of the window, closed his eyes and immediately fell asleep. I moved restlessly in my seat and then the man came out of the lavatory, not so urgently now, and with obvious peace of mind. I closed the door for him.

I stood up and stretched and this stretching of my limbs seemed to set in motion a stretching of the mind and I found myself thinking: 'I am in no hurry to get to Saharanpur and I have always wanted to see Shamli behind the station walls. If I get down now, I can spend the day here. It will be better than sitting in this train for another hour. Then in the evening I can catch the next train home.'

In those days I never had the patience to wait for second thoughts and so I began pulling my small suitcase out from under the seat.

The farmer woke up and asked, 'What are you doing, brother?'

'I'm getting out,' I said.

He went to sleep again.

It would have taken at least fifteen minutes to reach the door as people and their belongings cluttered up the passage. So I let my suitcase down from the window and followed it on to the platform.

There was no one to collect my ticket at the barrier because there was obviously no point in keeping a man there to collect tickets from passengers who never came. And anyway, I had a through-ticket to my destination which I would need in the evening.

I went out of the station and came to Shamli.

Outside the station there was a neem tree and under it

stood a tonga. The pony was nibbling at the grass at the foot of the tree. The youth in the front seat was the only human in sight. There were no signs of inhabitants or habitation. I approached the tonga and the youth stared at me as though he couldn't believe his eyes.

'Where is Shamli?' I asked.

'Why, friend, this is Shamli,' he said.

I looked around again but couldn't see any sign of life. A dusty road led past the station and disappeared into the forest.

'Does anyone live here?' I asked.

'I live here,' he said with an engaging smile. He looked an amiable, happy-go-lucky fellow. He wore a cotton tunic and dirty white pyjamas.

'Where?' I asked.

'In my tonga, of course,' he said. 'I have had this pony five years now. I carry supplies to the hotel. But today the manager has not come to collect them. You are going to the hotel? I will take you.'

'Oh, so there's a hotel?'

'Well, friend, it is called that. And there are a few houses too and some shops, but they are all about a mile from the station. If they were not a mile from here, I would be out of business.'

I felt relieved but I still had the feeling of having walked into a town consisting of one station, one pony and one man.

'You can take me,' I said. 'I'm staying till this evening.'

He heaved my suitcase into the seat beside him and I climbed in at the back. He flicked the reins and slapped his pony on the buttocks and, with a roll and a lurch, the buggy moved off down the dusty forest road.

'What brings you here?' asked the youth.

'Nothing,' I said. 'The train was delayed. I was feeling bored. And so I got off.'

He did not believe that but he didn't question me further. The sun was reaching up over the forest but the road lay in the shadow of tall trees—eucalyptus, mango and neem.

'Not many people stay in the hotel,' he said. 'So it is cheap. You will get a room for five rupees.'

'Who is the manager?'

'Mr Satish Dayal. It is his father's property. Satish Dayal could not pass his exams or get a job so his father sent him here to look after the hotel.'

The jungle thinned out and we passed a temple, a mosque, a few small shops. There was a strong smell of burnt sugar in the air and in the distance I saw a factory chimney. That, then, was the reason for Shamli's existence. We passed a bullock cart laden with sugarcane. The road went through fields of cane and maize, and then, just as we were about to re-enter the jungle, the youth pulled his horse to a side road and the hotel came in sight.

It was a small white bungalow with a garden in the front, banana trees at the sides and an orchard of guava trees at the back. We came jingling up to the front veranda. Nobody appeared, nor was there any sign of life on the premises.

'They are all asleep,' said the youth.

I said, 'I'll sit in the veranda and wait.' I got down from the tonga and the youth dropped my case on the veranda steps. Then he stooped in front of me, smiling amiably, waiting to be paid.

'Well, how much?' I asked.

'As a friend, only one rupee.'

'That's too much,' I complained. 'This is not Delhi.'

'This is Shamli,' he said. 'I am the only tonga in Shamli. You may not pay me anything, if that is your wish. But then, I will not take you back to the station this evening. You will have to walk.'

I gave him the rupee. He had both charm and cunning, an effective combination.

'Come in the evening at about six,' I said.

'I will come,' he said with an infectious smile. 'Don't worry.' I waited till the tonga had gone round the bend in the road before walking up the veranda steps.

The doors of the house were closed and there were no bells to ring. I didn't have a watch but I judged the time to be a little past six o'clock. The hotel didn't look very impressive. The whitewash was coming off the walls and the cane chairs on the veranda were old and crooked. A stag's head was mounted over the front door but one of its glass eyes had fallen out. I had often heard hunters speak of how beautiful an animal looked before it died, but how could anyone with true love of the beautiful care for the stuffed head of an animal, grotesquely mounted, with no resemblance to its living aspect?

I felt too restless to take any of the chairs. I began pacing up and down the veranda, wondering if I should start banging on the doors. Perhaps the hotel was deserted. Perhaps the tonga driver had played a trick on me. I began to regret my impulsiveness in leaving the train. When I saw the manager I would have to invent a reason for coming to his hotel. I was good at inventing reasons. I would tell him that a friend of mine had stayed here some years ago and that I was trying to trace him. I decided that my friend would have to be a little eccentric (having chosen Shamli to live in), that he had become a recluse, shutting himself off from the world. His parents—no, his sister—for his parents would be dead—had asked me to find him if I could and, as he had last been heard of in Shamli, I had taken the opportunity to inquire after him. His name would be Major Roberts, retired.

I heard a tap running at the side of the building and

walking around found a young man bathing at the tap. He was strong and well-built and slapped himself on the body with great enthusiasm. He had not seen me approaching so I waited until he had finished bathing and had begun to dry himself.

'Hallo,' I said.

He turned at the sound of my voice and looked at me for a few moments with a puzzled expression. He had a round cheerful face and crisp black hair. He smiled slowly. But it was a more genuine smile than the tonga driver's. So far I had met two people in Shamli and they were both smilers. That should have cheered me, but it didn't. 'You have come to stay?' he asked in a slow, easy-going voice.

'Just for the day,' I said. 'You work here?'

'Yes, my name is Daya Ram. The manager is asleep just now but I will find a room for you.'

He pulled on his vest and pyjamas and accompanied me back to the veranda. Here he picked up my suitcase and, unlocking a side door, led me into the house. We went down a passageway. Then Daya Ram stopped at the door on the right, pushed it open and took me into a small, sunny room that had a window looking out on to the orchard. There was a bed, a desk, a couple of cane chairs, and a frayed and faded red carpet.

'Is it all right?' said Daya Ram.

'Perfectly all right.'

'They have breakfast at eight o'clock. But if you are hungry, I will make something for you now.'

'No, it's all right. Are you the cook too?'

'I do everything here.'

'Do you like it?'

'No,' he said. And then added, in a sudden burst of confidence, 'There are no women for a man like me.'

'Why don't you leave, then?'

'I will,' he said with a doubtful look on his face. 'I will leave ...'

After he had gone I shut the door and went into the bathroom to bathe. The cold water refreshed me and made me feel one with the world. After I had dried myself, I sat on the bed, in front of the open window. A cool breeze, smelling of rain, came through the window and played over my body. I thought I saw a movement among the trees.

And getting closer to the window, I saw a girl on a swing. She was a small girl, all by herself, and she was swinging to and fro and singing, and her song carried faintly on the breeze.

I dressed quickly and left my room. The girl's dress was billowing in the breeze, her pigtails flying about. When she saw me approaching, she stopped swinging and stared at me. I stopped a little distance away.

'Who are you?' she asked.

'A ghost,' I replied.

'You look like one,' she said.

I decided to take this as a compliment, as I was determined to make friends. I did not smile at her because some children dislike adults who smile at them all the time.

'What's your name?' I asked.

'Kiran,' she said. 'I'm ten.'

'You are getting old.'

'Well, we all have to grow old one day. Aren't you coming any closer?'

'May I?' I asked.

'You may. You can push the swing.'

One pigtail lay across the girl's chest, the other behind her shoulder. She had a serious face and obviously felt she had responsibilities. She seemed to be in a hurry to grow up, and I suppose she had no time for anyone who treated her as a child. I pushed the swing until it went higher and higher and then I stopped pushing so that she came lower each time and we could talk.

'Tell me about the people who live here,' I said.

'There is Heera,' she said. 'He's the gardener. He's nearly a hundred. You can see him behind the hedges in the garden. You can't see him unless you look hard. He tells me stories, a new story every day. He's much better than the people in the hotel and so is Daya Ram.'

'Yes, I met Daya Ram.'

'He's my bodyguard. He brings me nice things from the kitchen when no one is looking.'

'You don't stay here?'

'No, I live in another house. You can't see it from here. My father is the manager of the factory.'

'Aren't there any other children to play with?' I asked.

'I don't know any,' she said.

'And the people staying here?'

'Oh, they.' Apparently Kiran didn't think much of the hotel guests. 'Miss Deeds is funny when she's drunk. And Mr Lin is the strangest.'

'And what about the manager, Mr Dayal?'

'He's mean. And he gets frightened of the slightest things. But Mrs Dayal is nice. She lets me take flowers home. But she doesn't talk much.'

I was fascinated by Kiran's ruthless summing up of the guests. I brought the swing to a standstill and asked, 'And what do you think of me?'

'I don't know as yet,' said Kiran quite seriously. 'I'll think about you.'

As I came back to the hotel, I heard the sound of a piano in one of the front rooms. I didn't know enough about music to be able to recognize the piece but it had sweetness and melody though it was played with some hesitancy. As

I came nearer, the sweetness deserted the music, probably because the piano was out of tune.

The person at the piano had distinctive Mongolian features and so I presumed he was Mr Lin. He hadn't seen me enter the room and I stood beside the curtains of the door, watching him play. He had full round lips and high, slanting cheekbones. His eyes were large and round and full of melancholy. His long, slender fingers hardly touched the keys.

I came nearer and then he looked up at me, without any show of surprise or displeasure, and kept on playing.

'What are you playing?' I asked.

'Chopin,' he said.

'Oh, yes. It's nice but the piano is fighting it.'

'I know. This piano belonged to one of Kipling's aunts. It hasn't been tuned since the last century.'

'Do you live here?'

'No, I come from Calcutta,' he answered readily. 'I have some business here with the sugarcane people, actually, though I am not a businessman.' He was playing softly all the time so that our conversation was not lost in the music. 'I don't know anything about business. But I have to do something.'

'Where did you learn to play the piano?'

'In Singapore. A French lady taught me. She had great hopes of my becoming a concert pianist when I grew up. I would have toured Europe and America.'

'Why didn't you?'

'We left during the War and I had to give up my lessons.'

'And why did you go to Calcutta?'

'My father is a Calcutta businessman. What do you do and why do you come here?' he asked. 'If I am not being too inquisitive.'

Before I could answer, a bell rang, loud and continuously, drowning the music and conversation.

'Breakfast,' said Mr Lin.

A thin dark man, wearing glasses, stepped nervously into the room and peered at me in an anxious manner.

'You arrived last night?'

'That's right,' I said. 'I just want to stay the day. I think you're the manager?'

'Yes. Would you like to sign the register?'

I went with him past the bar and into the office. I wrote my name and Mussoorie address in the register and the duration of my stay. I paused at the column marked 'Profession', thought it would be best to fill it with something and wrote 'Author'.

'You are here on business?' asked Mr Dayal.

'No, not exactly. You see, I'm looking for a friend of mine who was last heard of in Shamli, about three years ago. I thought I'd make a few inquiries in case he's still here.'

'What was his name? Perhaps he stayed here.'

'Major Roberts,' I said. 'An Anglo-Indian.'

'Well, you can look through the old registers after breakfast.'

He accompanied me into the dining room. The establishment was really more of a boarding house than a hotel because Mr Dayal ate with his guests. There was a round mahogany dining table in the centre of the room and Mr Lin was the only one seated at it. Daya Ram hovered about with plates and trays. I took my seat next to Lin and, as I did so, a door opened from the passage and a woman of about thirty-five came in.

She had on a skirt and blouse which accentuated a firm, well-rounded figure, and she walked on high heels, with a rhythmical swaying of the hips. She had an uninteresting face, camouflaged with lipstick, rouge and powder—the powder so thick that it had become embedded in the natural lines of her face—but her figure compelled admiration.

'Miss Deeds,' whispered Lin.

There was a false note to her greeting.

'Hallo, everyone,' she said heartily, straining for effect. 'Why are you all so quiet? Has Mr Lin been playing the Funeral March again?' She sat down and continued talking. 'Really, we must have a dance or something to liven things up. You must know some good numbers, Lin, after your experience of Singapore nightclubs. What's for breakfast? Boiled eggs. Daya Ram, can't you make an omelette for a change? I know you're not a professional cook but you don't have to give us the same thing every day, and there's absolutely no reason why you should burn the toast. You'll have to do something about a cook, Mr Dayal.' Then she noticed me sitting opposite her. 'Oh, hallo,' she said, genuinely surprised. She gave me a long appraising look.

'This gentleman,' said Mr Dayal introducing me, 'is an author.'

'That's nice,' said Miss Deeds. 'Are you married?'

'No,' I said. 'Are you?'

'Funny, isn't it,' she said, without taking offence, 'no one in this house seems to be married.'

'I'm married,' said Mr Dayal.

'Oh, yes, of course,' said Miss Deeds. 'And what brings you to Shamli?' she asked, turning to me.

'I'm looking for a friend called Major Roberts.'

Lin gave an exclamation of surprise. I thought he had seen through my deception.

But another game had begun.

'I knew him,' said Lin. 'A great friend of mine.'

'Yes,' continued Lin. 'I knew him. A good chap, Major Roberts.'

Well, there I was, inventing people to suit my convenience, and people like Mr Lin started inventing relationships with them. I was too intrigued to try and discourage him. I wanted to see how far he would go.

'When did you meet him?' asked Lin, taking the initiative.

'Oh, only about three years back, just before he disappeared. He was last heard of in Shamli.'

'Yes, I heard he was here,' said Lin. 'But he went away, when he thought his relatives had traced him. He went into the mountains near Tibet.'

'Did he?' I said, unwilling to be instructed further. 'What part of the country? I come from the hills myself. I know the Mana and Niti passes quite well. If you have any idea of exactly where he went, I think I could find him.' I had the advantage in this exchange because I was the one who had originally invented Roberts. Yet I couldn't bring myself to end his deception, probably because I felt sorry for him. A happy man wouldn't take the trouble of inventing friendships with people who didn't exist. He'd be too busy with friends who did.

'You've had a lonely life, Mr Lin?' I asked.

'Lonely?' said Mr Lin, with forced incredulousness. 'I'd never been lonely till I came here a month ago. When I was in Singapore ...'

'You never get any letters though, do you?' asked Miss Deeds suddenly.

Lin was silent for a moment. Then he said: 'Do you?'

Miss Deeds lifted her head a little, as a horse does when it is annoyed, and I thought her pride had been hurt, but then she laughed unobtrusively and tossed her head.

'I never write letters,' she said. 'My friends gave me up as hopeless years ago. They know it's no use writing to me because they rarely get a reply. They call me the Jungle Princess.'

Mr Dayal tittered and I found it hard to suppress a smile. To cover up my smile I asked, 'You teach here?'

'Yes, I teach at the girls' school,' she said with a frown. 'But don't talk to me about teaching. I have enough of it all day.'

'You don't like teaching?'

She gave me an aggressive look. 'Should I?' she asked.

'Shouldn't you?' I said.

She paused, and then said, 'Who are you, anyway, the Inspector of Schools?'

'No,' said Mr Dayal who wasn't following very well, 'he's a journalist.'

'I've heard they are nosey,' said Miss Deeds.

Once again Lin interrupted to steer the conversation away from a delicate issue.

'Where's Mrs Dayal this morning?' asked Lin.

'She spent the night with our neighbours,' said Mr Dayal. 'She should be here after lunch.'

It was the first time Mrs Dayal had been mentioned. Nobody spoke either well or ill of her. I suspected that she kept her distance from the others, avoiding familiarity. I began to wonder about Mrs Dayal.

Daya Ram came in from the veranda looking worried.

'Heera's dog has disappeared,' he said. 'He thinks a leopard took it.'

Heera, the gardener, was standing respectfully outside on the veranda steps. We all hurried out to him, firing questions which he didn't try to answer.

'Yes. It's a leopard,' said Kiran appearing from behind Heera. 'It's going to come into the hotel,' she added cheerfully.

'Be quiet,' said Satish Dayal crossly.

'There are pug marks under the trees,' said Daya Ram.

Mr Dayal, who seemed to know little about leopards or pug marks, said, 'I will take a look,' and led the way to the orchard, the rest of us trailing behind in an ill-assorted procession.

There were marks on the soft earth in the orchard (they could have been a leopard's) which went in the direction of the riverbed. Mr Dayal paled a little and went hurrying back to the hotel. Heera returned to the front garden, the least excited, the most sorrowful. Everyone else was thinking of a leopard but he was thinking of the dog.

I followed him and watched him weeding the sunflower beds. His face was wrinkled like a walnut but his eyes were clear and bright. His hands were thin and bony but there was a deftness and power in the wrist and fingers and the weeds flew fast from his spade. He had cracked, parchment-like skin. I could not help thinking of the gloss and glow of Daya Ram's limbs as I had seen them when he was bathing and wondered if Heera's had once been like that and if Daya Ram's would ever be like this, and both possibilities—or were they probabilities—saddened me. Our skin, I thought, is like the leaf of a tree, young and green and shiny. Then it gets darker and heavier, sometimes spotted with disease, sometimes eaten away. Then fading, yellow and red, then falling, crumbling into dust or feeding the flames of fire. I looked at my own skin, still smooth, not coarsened by labour. I thought of Kiran's fresh rose-tinted complexion; Miss Deeds' skin, hard and dry; Lin's pale taut skin, stretched tightly across his prominent cheeks and forehead; and Mr Dayal's grey skin growing thick hair. And I wondered about Mrs Dayal and the kind of skin she would have.

'Did you have the dog for long?' I asked Heera.

He looked up with surprise for he had been unaware of my presence.

'Six years, sahib,' he said. 'He was not a clever dog but he was very friendly. He followed me home one day when I was coming back from the bazaar. I kept telling him to go away but he wouldn't. It was a long walk and so I began talking to him. I liked talking to him and I have always talked to him and we have understood each other. That first night, when I came home I shut the gate between us. But he stood on the other side looking at me with trusting eyes. Why did he have to look at me like that?'

'So you kept him?'

'Yes, I could never forget the way he looked at me. I shall feel lonely now because he was my only companion. My wife and son died long ago. It seems I am to stay here forever, until everyone has gone, until there are only ghosts in Shamli. Already the ghosts are here . . .'

I heard a light footfall behind me and turned to find Kiran. The barefoot girl stood beside the gardener and with her toes began to pull at the weeds.

'You are a lazy one,' said the old man. 'If you want to help me sit down and use your hands.'

I looked at the girl's fair round face and in her bright eyes I saw something old and wise. And I looked into the old man's wise eyes, and saw something forever bright and young. The skin cannot change the eyes. The eyes are the true reflection of a man's age and sensibilities. Even a blind man has hidden eyes.

'I hope we find the dog,' said Kiran. 'But I would like a leopard. Nothing ever happens here.'

'Not now,' sighed Heera. 'Not now . . . Why, once there was a band and people danced till morning, but now . . .' He paused, lost in thought and then said: 'I have always been here. I was here before Shamli.'

'Before the station?'

'Before there was a station, or a factory, or a bazaar. It was a village then, and the only way to get here was by bullock cart. Then a bus service was started, then the railway lines were laid and a station built, then they started the sugar factory, and for a few years Shamli was a town. But the jungle was bigger than the town. The rains were heavy and malaria was everywhere. People didn't stay long in Shamli. Gradually, they went back into the hills.

*Ruskin Bond*

Sometimes I too wanted to go back to the hills, but what is the use when you are old and have no one left in the world except a few flowers in a troublesome garden. I had to choose between the flowers and the hills, and I chose the flowers. I am tired now, and old, but I am not tired of flowers.'

I could see that his real world was the garden; there was more variety in his flower beds than there was in the town of Shamli. Every month, every day, there were new flowers in the garden, but there were always the same people in Shamli.

I left Kiran with the old man, and returned to my room. It must have been about eleven o'clock.

I was facing the window when I heard my door being opened. Turning, I perceived the barrel of a gun moving slowly round the edge of the door. Behind the gun was Satish Dayal, looking hot and sweaty. I didn't know what his intentions were; so, deciding it would be better to act first and reason later, I grabbed a pillow from the bed and flung it in his face. I then threw myself at his legs and brought him crashing down to the ground.

When we got up, I was holding the gun. It was an old Enfield rifle, probably dating back to the Afghan wars, the kind that goes off at the least encouragement.

'But—but—why?' stammered the dishevelled and alarmed Mr Dayal.

'I don't know,' I said menacingly. 'Why did you come in here pointing this at me?'

'I wasn't pointing it at you. It's for the leopard.'

'Oh, so you came into my room looking for a leopard? You have, I presume been stalking one about the hotel?' (By now I was convinced that Mr Dayal had taken leave of his senses and was hunting imaginary leopards.)

'No, no,' cried the distraught man, becoming more

confused. 'I was looking for you. I wanted to ask you if you could use a gun. I was thinking we should go looking for the leopard that took Heera's dog. Neither Mr Lin nor I can shoot.'

'Your gun is not up-to-date,' I said. 'It's not at all suitable for hunting leopards. A stout stick would be more effective. Why don't we arm ourselves with lathis and make a general assault?'

I said this banteringly, but Mr Dayal took the idea quite seriously. 'Yes, yes,' he said with alacrity, 'Daya Ram has got one or two lathis in the godown. The three of us could make an expedition. I have asked Mr Lin but he says he doesn't want to have anything to do with leopards.'

'What about our Jungle Princess?' I said. 'Miss Deeds should be pretty good with a lathi.'

'Yes, yes,' said Mr Dayal humourlessly, 'but we'd better not ask her.'

Collecting Daya Ram and two lathis, we set off for the orchard and began following the pug marks through the trees. It took us ten minutes to reach the riverbed, a dry hot rocky place; then we went into the jungle, Mr Dayal keeping well to the rear. The atmosphere was heavy and humid, and there was not a breath of air amongst the trees. When a parrot squawked suddenly, shattering the silence, Mr Dayal let out a startled exclamation and started for home.

'What was that?' he asked nervously.

'A bird,' I explained.

'I think we should go back now,' he said. 'I don't think the leopard's here.'

'You never know with leopards,' I said, 'they could be anywhere.'

Mr Dayal stepped away from the bushes. 'I'll have to go,' he said. 'I have a lot of work. You keep a lathi with you, and I'll send Daya Ram back later.'

'That's very thoughtful of you,' I said.

Daya Ram scratched his head and reluctantly followed his employer back through the trees. I moved on slowly, down the little used path, wondering if I should also return. I saw two monkeys playing on the branch of a tree, and decided that there could be no danger in the immediate vicinity.

Presently I came to a clearing where there was a pool of fresh clear water. It was fed by a small stream that came suddenly, like a snake, out of the long grass. The water looked cool and inviting. Laying down the lathi and taking off my clothes, I ran down the bank until I was waist-deep in the middle of the pool. I splashed about for some time before emerging, then I lay on the soft grass and allowed the sun to dry my body. I closed my eyes and gave myself up to beautiful thoughts. I had forgotten all about leopards.

I must have slept for about half an hour because when I awoke, I found that Daya Ram had come back and was vigorously threshing about in the narrow confines of the pool. I sat up and asked him the time.

'Twelve o'clock,' he shouted, coming out of the water, his dripping body all gold and silver in sunlight. 'They will be waiting for dinner.'

'Let them wait,' I said.

It was a relief to talk to Daya Ram, after the uneasy conversations in the lounge and dining room.

'Dayal Sahib will be angry with me.'

'I'll tell him we found the trail of the leopard, and that we went so far into the jungle that we lost our way. As Miss Deeds is so critical of the food, let her cook the meal.'

'Oh, she only talks like that,' said Daya Ram. 'Inside she is very soft. She is too soft in some ways.'

'She should be married.'

'Well, she would like to be. Only there is no one to

marry her. When she came here she was engaged to be married to an English army captain. I think she loved him, but she is the sort of person who cannot help loving many men all at once, and the captain could not understand that—it is just the way she is made, I suppose. She is always ready to fall in love.'

'You seem to know,' I said.

'Oh, yes.'

We dressed and walked back to the hotel. In a few hours, I thought, the tonga will come for me and I will be back at the station. The mysterious charm of Shamli will be no more, but whenever I pass this way I will wonder about these people, about Miss Deeds and Lin and Mrs Dayal.

Mrs Dayal . . . She was the one person I had yet to meet. It was with some excitement and curiosity that I looked forward to meeting her; she was about the only mystery left in Shamli, now, and perhaps she would be no mystery when I met her. And yet . . . I felt that perhaps she would justify the impulse that made me get down from the train.

I could have asked Daya Ram about Mrs Dayal, and so satisfied my curiosity; but I wanted to discover her for myself. Half the day was left to me, and I didn't want my game to finish too early.

I walked towards the veranda, and the sound of the piano came through the open door.

'I wish Mr Lin would play something cheerful,' said Miss Deeds. 'He's obsessed with the Funeral March. Do you dance?'

'Oh, no,' I said.

She looked disappointed. But when Lin left the piano, she went into the lounge and sat down on the stool. I stood at the door watching her, wondering what she would do. Lin left the room somewhat resentfully.

*Ruskin Bond*

She began to play an old song which I remembered having heard in a film or on a gramophone record. She sang while she played, in a slightly harsh but pleasant voice:

*Rolling round the world*
*Looking for the sunshine*
*I know I'm going to find some day ...*

Then she played *Am I blue?* and *Darling, je vous aime beaucoup.* She sat there singing in a deep husky voice, her eyes a little misty, her hard face suddenly kind and sloppy. When the dinner gong rang, she broke off playing and shook off her sentimental mood, and laughed derisively at herself.

I don't remember that lunch. I hadn't slept much since the previous night and I was beginning to feel the strain of my journey. The swim had refreshed me, but it had also made me drowsy. I ate quite well, though, of rice and kofta curry, and then feeling sleepy, made for the garden to find a shady tree.

There were some books on the shelf in the lounge, and I ran my eye over them in search of one that might condition sleep. But they were too dull to do even that. So I went into the garden, and there was Kiran on the swing, and I went to her tree and sat down on the grass.

'Did you find the leopard?' she asked.

'No,' I said, with a yawn.

'Tell me a story.'

'You tell me one,' I said.

'All right. Once there was a lazy man with long legs, who was always yawning and wanting to fall asleep ...'

I watched the swaying motions of the swing and the movements of the girl's bare legs, and a tiny insect kept buzzing about in front of my nose ...

'... and fall asleep, and the reason for this was that he liked to dream.'

I blew the insect away, and the swing became hazy and distant, and Kiran was a blurred figure in the trees ...

'... liked to dream, and what do you think he dreamt about ...?' Dreamt about, dreamt about ...

When I awoke there was that cool rain-scented breeze blowing across the garden. I remember lying on the grass with my eyes closed, listening to the swishing of the swing. Either I had not slept long, or Kiran had been a long time on the swing; it was moving slowly now, in a more leisurely fashion, without much sound. I opened my eyes and saw that my arm was stained with the juice of the grass beneath me. Looking up, I expected to see Kiran's legs waving above me. But instead I saw dark slim feet and above them the folds of a sari. I straightened up against the trunk of the tree to look closer at Kiran, but Kiran wasn't there. It was someone else in the swing, a young woman in a pink sari, with a red rose in her hair.

She had stopped the swing with her foot on the ground, and she was smiling at me.

It wasn't a smile you could see, it was a tender fleeting movement that came suddenly and was gone at the same time, and its going was sad. I thought of the others' smiles, just as I had thought of their skins: the tonga driver's friendly, deceptive smile; Daya Ram's wide sincere smile; Miss Deeds' cynical, derisive smile. And looking at Sushila, I knew a smile could never change. She had always smiled that way.

'You haven't changed,' she said.

I was standing up now, though still leaning against the tree for support. Though I had never thought much about the sound of her voice, it seemed as familiar as the sounds of yesterday.

'You haven't changed either,' I said. 'But where did you come from?' I wasn't sure yet if I was awake or dreaming.

She laughed as she had always laughed at me.

'I came from behind the tree. The little girl has gone.'

'Yes, I'm dreaming,' I said helplessly.

'But what brings you here?'

'I don't know. At least I didn't know when I came. But it must have been you. The train stopped at Shamli and I don't know why, but I decided I would spend the day here, behind the station walls. You must be married now, Sushila.'

'Yes, I am married to Mr Dayal, the manager of the hotel. And what has been happening to you?'

'I am still a writer, still poor, and still living in Mussoorie.'

'When were you last in Delhi?' she asked. 'I don't mean Delhi, I mean at home.'

'I have not been to your home since you were there.'

'Oh, my friend,' she said, getting up suddenly and coming to me, 'I want to talk about our home and Sunil and our friends and all those things that are so far away now. I have been here two years, and I am already feeling old. I keep remembering our home—how young I was, how happy—and I am all alone with memories. But now you are here! It was a bit of magic. I came through the trees after Kiran had gone, and there you were, fast asleep under the tree. I didn't wake you then because I wanted to see you wake up.'

'As I used to watch you wake up . . .'

She was near me and I could look at her more closely. Her cheeks did not have the same freshness—they were a little pale—and she was thinner now, but her eyes were the same, smiling the same way. Her fingers, when she took my hand, were the same warm delicate fingers.

'Talk to me,' she said. 'Tell me about yourself.'

'You tell me,' I said.

'I am here,' she said. 'That is all there is to say about myself.'

'Then let us sit down and I'll talk.'

'Not here,' she took my hand and led me through the trees. 'Come with me.'

I heard the jingle of a tonga bell and a faint shout. I stopped and laughed.

'My tonga,' I said. 'It has come to take me back to the station.'

'But you are not going,' said Sushila, immediately downcast.

'I will tell him to come in the morning,' I said. 'I will spend the night in your Shamli.'

I walked to the front of the hotel where the tonga was waiting. I was glad no one else was in sight. The youth was smiling at me in his most appealing manner.

'I'm not going today,' I said. 'Will you come tomorrow morning?'

'I can come whenever you like, friend. But you will have to pay for every trip, because it is a long way from the station even if my tonga is empty. Usual fare, friend, one rupee.'

I didn't try to argue but resignedly gave him the rupee. He cracked his whip and pulled on the reins, and the carriage moved off.

'If you don't leave tomorrow,' the youth called out after me, 'you'll never leave Shamli!'

I walked back through the trees, but I couldn't find Sushila.

'Sushila, where are you?' I called, but I might have been speaking to the trees, for I had no reply. There was a small path going through the orchard, and on the path I saw a rose petal. I walked a little further and saw another petal. They were from Sushila's red rose. I walked on down the path until I had skirted the orchard, and then the path went along the fringe of the jungle, past a clump of bamboos, and here the grass was a lush green as though it had been constantly watered. I was still finding rose petals. I heard the chatter of seven sisters, and the call of a hoopoe. The path bent to meet a stream, there was a willow coming down to the water's edge, and Sushila was waiting there.

'Why didn't you wait?' I said.

'I wanted to see if you were as good at following me as you used to be.'

'Well, I am,' I said, sitting down beside her on the grassy bank of the stream. 'Even if I'm out of practice.'

'Yes, I remember the time you climbed up an apple tree to pick some fruit for me. You got up all right but then you couldn't come down again. I had to climb up myself and help you.'

'I don't remember that,' I said.

'Of course you do.'

'It must have been your other friend, Pramod.'

'I never climbed trees with Pramod.'

'Well, I don't remember.'

I looked at the little stream that ran past us. The water was no more than ankle-deep, cold and clear and sparking, like the mountain stream near my home. I took off my shoes, rolled up my trousers, and put my feet in the water. Sushila's feet joined mine.

At first I had wanted to ask about her marriage, whether she was happy or not, what she thought of her husband; but now I couldn't ask her these things. They seemed far away and of little importance. I could think of nothing she had in common with Mr Dayal. I felt that her charm and attractiveness and warmth could not have been appreciated, or even noticed, by that curiously distracted man. He was much older than her, of course, probably older than me. He was obviously not her choice but her parents', and so far they were childless. Had there been children, I don't think Sushila would have minded Mr Dayal as her husband. Children would have made up for the absence of passion— or was there passion in Satish Dayal? ... I remembered having heard that Sushila had been married to a man she didn't like. I remembered having shrugged off the news, because it meant she would never come my way again, and I have never yearned after something that has been irredeemably lost. But she had come my way again. And was she still lost? That was what I wanted to know ...

'What do you do with yourself all day?' I asked.

'Oh, I visit the school and help with the classes. It is the only interest I have in this place. The hotel is terrible. I try to keep away from it as much as I can.'

'And what about the guests?'

'Oh, don't let us talk about them. Let us talk about ourselves. Do you have to go tomorrow?'

'Yes, I suppose so. Will you always be in this place?'

'I suppose so.'

That made me silent. I took her hand, and my feet churned up the mud at the bottom of the stream. As the mud subsided, I saw Sushila's face reflected in the water, and looking up at her again, into her dark eyes, the old yearning returned and I wanted to care for her and protect her. I wanted to take her away from that place, from sorrowful Shamli. I wanted her to live again. Of course, I had forgotten all about my poor finances, Sushila's family, and the shoes I wore, which were my last pair. The uplift I was experiencing in this meeting with Sushila, who had always, throughout her childhood and youth, bewitched me as no other had ever bewitched me, made me reckless and impulsive.

I lifted her hand to my lips and kissed her on the soft of her palm.

'Can I kiss you?' I said.

'You have just done so.'

'Can I kiss you?' I repeated.

'It is not necessary.'

I leaned over and kissed her slender neck. I knew she would like this, because that was where I had kissed her often before. I kissed her on the soft of the throat, where it tickled.

'It is not necessary,' she said, but she ran her fingers through my hair and let them rest there. I kissed her behind the ear then, and kept my mouth to her ear and whispered, 'Can I kiss you?'

She turned her face to me so that we looked deep into each other's eyes, and I kissed her again. And we put our arms around each other and lay together on the grass with the water running over our feet. We said nothing at all, simply lay there for what seemed like several years, or until the first drop of rain.

It was a big wet drop, and it splashed on Sushila's cheek just next to mine, and ran down to her lips so that I had to kiss her again. The next big drop splattered on the tip of my nose, and Sushila laughed and sat up. Little ringlets were forming on the stream where the raindrops hit the water, and above us there was a pattering on the banana leaves.

'We must go,' said Sushila.

We started homewards, but had not gone far before it was raining steadily, and Sushila's hair came loose and streamed down her body. The rain fell harder, and we had to hop over pools and avoid the soft mud. Sushila's sari was plastered to her body, accentuating her ripe, thrusting breasts, and I was excited to passion. I pulled her beneath a big tree, crushed her in my arms and kissed her rain-kissed mouth. And then I thought she was crying, but I wasn't sure, because it might have been the raindrops on her cheeks.

'Come away with me,' I said. 'Leave this place. Come away with me tomorrow morning. We will go somewhere where nobody will know us or come between us.'

She smiled at me and said, 'You are still a dreamer, aren't you?'

'Why can't you come?'

'I am married. It is as simple as that.'

'If it is that simple you can come.'

'I have to think of my parents, too. It would break my father's heart if I were to do what you are proposing. And you are proposing it without a thought for the consequences.'

'You are too practical,' I said.

'If women were not practical, most marriages would be failures.'

'So your marriage is a success?'

'Of course it is, as a marriage. I am not happy and I do not love him, but neither am I so unhappy that I should hate him. Sometimes, for our own sakes, we have to think of the happiness of others. What happiness would we have living in hiding from everyone we once knew and cared for. Don't be a fool. I am always here and you can come to see me, and nobody will be made unhappy by it. But take me away and we will only have regrets.'

'You don't love me,' I said foolishly.

'That sad word love,' she said, and became pensive and silent.

I could say no more. I was angry again and rebellious, and there was no one and nothing to rebel against. I could not understand someone who was afraid to break away from an unhappy existence lest that existence should become unhappier. I had always considered it an admirable thing to break away from security and respectability. Of course, it is easier for a man to do this. A man can look after himself, he can do without neighbours and the approval of

*Ruskin Bond*

the local society. A woman, I reasoned, would do anything for love provided it was not at the price of security; for a woman loves security as much as a man loves independence.

'I must go back now,' said Sushila. 'You follow a little later.'

'All you wanted to do was talk,' I complained.

She laughed at that and pulled me playfully by the hair. Then she ran out from under the tree, springing across the grass, and the wet mud flew up and flecked her legs. I watched her through the thin curtain of rain until she reached the veranda. She turned to wave to me, and then skipped into the hotel.

The rain had lessened, but I didn't know what to do with myself. The hotel was uninviting, and it was too late to leave Shamli. If the grass hadn't been wet I would have preferred to sleep under a tree rather than return to the hotel to sit at that alarming dining table.

I came out from under the trees and crossed the garden. But instead of making for the veranda I went round to the back of the hotel. Smoke issuing from the barred window of a back room told me I had probably found the kitchen. Daya Ram was inside, squatting in front of a stove, stirring a pot of stew. The stew smelt appetizing. Daya Ram looked up and smiled at me.

'I thought you had gone,' he said.

'I'll go in the morning,' I said, pulling myself up on an empty table. Then I had one of my sudden ideas and said, 'Why don't you come with me? I can find you a good job in Mussoorie. How much do you get paid here?'

'Fifty rupees a month. But I haven't been paid for three months.'

'Could you get your pay before tomorrow morning?'

'No, I won't get anything until one of the guests pays a bill. Miss Deeds owes about fifty rupees on whisky alone.

She will pay up, she says, when the school pays her salary. And the school can't pay her until they collect the children's fees. That is how bankrupt everyone is in Shamli.'

'I see,' I said, though I didn't see. 'But Mr Dayal can't hold back your pay just because his guests haven't paid their bills.'

'He can if he hasn't got any money.'

'I see,' I said. 'Anyway, I will give you my address. You can come when you are free.'

'I will take it from the register,' he said.

I edged over to the stove and leaning over, sniffed at the stew. 'I'll eat mine now,' I said. And without giving Daya Ram a chance to object, I lifted a plate off the shelf, took hold of the stirring spoon and helped myself from the pot.

'There's rice too,' said Daya Ram.

I filled another plate with rice and then got busy with my fingers. After ten minutes I had finished. I sat back comfortably, in a ruminative mood. With my stomach full I could take a more tolerant view of life and people. I could understand Sushila's apprehensions, Lin's delicate lying and Miss Deeds' aggressiveness. Daya Ram went out to sound the dinner gong, and I trailed back to my room.

From the window of my room I saw Kiran running across the lawn and I called to her, but she didn't hear me. She ran down the path and out of the gate, her pigtails beating against the wind.

The clouds were breaking and coming together again, twisting and spiralling their way across a violet sky. The sun was going down behind the Siwaliks. The sky there was bloodshot. The tall slim trunks of the eucalyptus tree were tinged with an orange glow; the rain had stopped, and the wind was a soft, sullen puff, drifting sadly through the trees. There was a steady drip of water from the eaves of the roof on to the window sill. Then the sun went down behind the old, old hills, and I remembered my own hills, far beyond these.

The room was dark but I did not turn on the light. I stood near the window, listening to the garden. There was a frog warbling somewhere and there was a sudden flap of wings overhead. Tomorrow morning I would go, and perhaps I would come back to Shamli one day, and perhaps not. I could always come here looking for Major Roberts, and who knows, one day I might find him. What should he be like, this lost man? A romantic, a man with a dream, a man with brown skin and blue eyes, living in a hut on a snowy mountain top, chopping wood and catching fish and swimming in cold mountain streams; a rough, free man with a kind heart and a shaggy beard, a man who owed allegiance to no one, who gave a damn for money and politics, and cities and civilizations, who was his own master, who lived at one with nature knowing no fear. But that was not Major Roberts—that was the man I wanted to be. He was not a Frenchman or an Englishman, he was me, a dream of myself. If only I could find Major Roberts.

When Daya Ram knocked on the door and told me the others had finished dinner, I left my room and made for the lounge. It was quite lively in the lounge. Satish Dayal was at the bar, Lin at the piano, and Miss Deeds in the centre of the room executing a tango on her own. It was obvious she had been drinking heavily.

'All on credit,' complained Mr Dayal to me. 'I don't know when I'll be paid, but I don't dare refuse her anything for fear she starts breaking up the hotel.'

'She could do that, too,' I said. 'It would come down without much encouragement.'

Lin began to play a waltz (I think it was a waltz), and then I found Miss Deeds in front of me, saying, 'Wouldn't you like to dance, old boy?'

'Thank you,' I said, somewhat alarmed. 'I hardly know how to.'

'Oh, come on, be a sport,' she said, pulling me away from the bar. I was glad Sushila wasn't present. She wouldn't have minded, but she'd have laughed as she always laughed when I made a fool of myself.

We went around the floor in what I suppose was waltz time, though all I did was mark time to Miss Deeds' motions. We were not very steady—this because I was trying to keep her at arm's length, while she was determined to have me crushed to her bosom. At length Lin finished the waltz. Giving him a grateful look, I pulled myself free. Miss Deeds went over to the piano, leaned right across it and said, 'Play something lively, dear Mr Lin, play some hot stuff.'

To my surprise Mr Lin without so much as an expression of distaste or amusement, began to execute what I suppose was the frug or the jitterbug. I was glad she hadn't asked me to dance that one with her.

It all appeared very incongruous to me: Miss Deeds letting herself go in crazy abandonment, Lin playing the piano with great seriousness, and Mr Dayal watching from the bar with an anxious frown. I wondered what Sushila would have thought of them now.

Eventually Miss Deeds collapsed on the couch breathing heavily. 'Give me a drink,' she cried.

With the noblest of intentions I took her a glass of water. Miss Deeds took a sip and made a face. 'What's this stuff?' she asked. 'It is different.'

'Water,' I said.

'No,' she said, 'now don't joke, tell me what it is.'

'It's water, I assure you,' I said.

When she saw that I was serious, her face coloured up and I thought she would throw the water at me. But she was too tired to do this and contented herself with throwing the glass over her shoulder. Mr Dayal made a dive for the flying glass, but he wasn't in time to rescue it and it hit the wall and fell to pieces on the floor.

Mr Dayal wrung his hands. 'You'd better take her to her room,' he said, as though I were personally responsible for her behaviour just because I'd danced with her.

'I can't carry her alone,' I said, making an unsuccessful attempt at helping Miss Deeds up from the couch.

Mr Dayal called for Daya Ram, and the big amiable youth came lumbering into the lounge. We took an arm each and helped Miss Deeds, feet dragging, across the room. We got her to her room and on to her bed. When we were about to withdraw she said, 'Don't go, my dear, stay with me a little while.'

Daya Ram had discreetly slipped outside. With my hand on the doorknob I said, 'Which of us?'

'Oh, are there two of you?' said Miss Deeds, without a trace of disappointment.

'Yes, Daya Ram helped me carry you here.'

'Oh, and who are you?'

'I'm the writer. You danced with me, remember?'

'Of course. You dance divinely, Mr Writer. Do stay with me. Daya Ram can stay too if he likes.'

I hesitated, my hand on the doorknob. She hadn't opened her eyes all the time I'd been in the room, her arms hung loose, and one bare leg hung over the side of the bed. She was fascinating somehow, and desirable, but I was afraid of her. I went out of the room and quietly closed the door.

As I lay awake in bed I heard the jackal's 'Pheau', the cry of fear which it communicates to all the jungle when there is danger about, a leopard or a tiger. It was a weird howl, and between each note there was a kind of low gurgling. I switched off the light and peered through the closed window. I saw the jackal at the edge of the lawn. It sat almost vertically on its haunches, holding its head straight up to the sky, making the neighbourhood vibrate with the eerie violence of its cries. Then suddenly it started up and ran off into the trees.

Before getting back into bed I made sure the window was shut. The bullfrog was singing again, 'ing-ong, ing-ong', in some foreign language. I wondered if Sushila was awake too, thinking about me. It must have been almost eleven o'clock. I thought of Miss Deeds with her leg hanging over the edge of the bed. I tossed restlessly and then sat up. I hadn't slept for two nights but I was not sleepy. I got out of bed without turning on the light and slowly opening my door, crept down the passageway. I stopped at the door of Miss Deeds' room. I stood there listening, but I heard only the ticking of the big clock that might have been in the room or somewhere in the passage. I put my hand on the doorknob, but the door was bolted. That settled the matter.

I would definitely leave Shamli the next morning. Another day in the company of these people and I would be behaving like them. Perhaps I was already doing so! I remembered the tonga driver's words: 'Don't stay too long in Shamli or you will never leave!'

When the rain came, it was not with a preliminary patter or shower, but all at once, sweeping across the forest like a massive wall, and I could hear it in the trees long before it reached the house. Then it came crashing down on the corrugated roof, and the hailstones hit the window panes with a hard metallic sound so that I thought the glass would break. The sound of thunder was like the booming of big guns and the lightning kept playing over the garden. At every flash of lightning I sighted the swing under the tree, rocking and leaping in the air as though some invisible, agitated being was sitting on it. I wondered about Kiran. Was she sleeping through all this, blissfully unconcerned, or was she lying awake in bed, starting at every clash of thunder as I was? Or was she up and about, exulting in the storm? I half expected to see her come running through the trees, through the rain, to stand on the swing with her hair blowing wild in the wind, laughing at the thunder and the angry skies. Perhaps I did see her, perhaps she was there. I wouldn't have been surprised if she were some forest nymph living in the hole of a tree, coming out sometimes to play in the garden.

A crash, nearer and louder than any thunder so far, made me sit up in bed with a start. Perhaps lightning had struck the house. I turned on the switch but the light didn't come on. A tree must have fallen across the line.

I heard voices in the passage—the voices of several people. I stepped outside to find out what had happened, and started at the appearance of a ghostly apparition right in front of me. It was Mr Dayal standing on the threshold in an oversized pyjama suit, a candle in his hand.

'I came to wake you,' he said. 'This storm . . .'

He had the irritating habit of stating the obvious.

'Yes, the storm,' I said. 'Why is everybody up?'

'The back wall has collapsed and part of the roof has fallen in. We'd better spend the night in the lounge—it is the safest room. This is a very old building,' he added apologetically.

'All right,' I said. 'I am coming.'

The lounge was lit by two candles. One stood over the piano, the other on a small table near the couch. Miss Deeds was on the couch, Lin was at the piano stool, looking as though he would start playing Stravinsky any moment, and Dayal was fussing about the room. Sushila was standing at a window, looking out at the stormy night. I went to the window and touched her but she didn't look around or say anything. The lightning flashed and her dark eyes were pools of smouldering fire.

'What time will you be leaving?' she asked.

'The tonga will come for me at seven.'

'If I come,' she said, 'if I come with you, I will be at the station before the train leaves.'

'How will you get there?' I asked, and hope and excitement rushed over me again.

'I will get there,' she said. 'I will get there before you. But if I am not there, then do not wait, do not come back for me. Go on your way. It will mean I do not want to come. Or I will be there.'

'But are you sure?'

'Don't stand near me now. Don't speak to me unless you have to.' She squeezed my fingers, then drew her hand away. I sauntered over to the next window, then back into the centre of the room. A gust of wind blew through a cracked windowpane and put out the candle near the couch.

'Damn the wind,' said Miss Deeds.

The window in my room had burst open during the night and there were leaves and branches strewn about the floor. I sat down on the damp bed and smelt eucalyptus. The earth was red, as though the storm had bled it all night.

After a little while I went into the veranda with my suitcase to wait for the tonga. It was then that I saw Kiran under the trees. Kiran's long black pigtails were tied up in a red ribbon, and she looked fresh and clean like the rain and the red earth. She stood looking seriously at me.

'Did you like the storm?' she asked.

'Some of the time,' I said. 'I'm going soon. Can I do anything for you?'

'Where are you going?'

'I'm going to the end of the world. I'm looking for Major Roberts, have you seen him anywhere?'

'There is no Major Roberts,' she said perceptively. 'Can I come with you to the end of the world?'

'What about your parents?'

'Oh, we won't take them.'

'They might be annoyed if you go off on your own.'

'I can stay on my own. I can go anywhere.'

'Well, one day I'll come back here and I'll take you everywhere and no one will stop us. Now is there anything else I can do for you?'

'I want some flowers, but I can't reach them,' she pointed to a hibiscus tree that grew against the wall. It meant climbing the wall to reach the flowers. Some of the red flowers had fallen during the night and were floating in a pool of water.

'All right,' I said and pulled myself up on the wall. I smiled down into Kiran's serious, upturned face. 'I'll throw them to you and you can catch them.'

I bent a branch, but the wood was young and green and I had to twist it several times before it snapped.

'I hope nobody minds,' I said, as I dropped the flowering branch to Kiran.

'It's nobody's tree,' she said.

'Sure?'

She nodded vigorously. 'Sure, don't worry.'

I was working for her and she felt immensely capable of protecting me. Talking and being with Kiran, I felt a nostalgic longing for childhood—emotions that had been beautiful because they were never completely understood.

'Who is your best friend?' I said.

'Daya Ram,' she replied. 'I told you so before.'

She was certainly faithful to her friends.

'And who is the second best?'

She put her finger in her mouth to consider the question, and her head dropped sideways.

'I'll make you the second best,' she said.

I dropped the flowers over her head. 'That is so kind of you. I'm proud to be your second best.'

I heard the tonga bell, and from my perch on the wall

saw the carriage coming down the driveway. 'That's for me,' I said. 'I must go now.'

I jumped down the wall. And the sole of my shoe came off at last.

'I knew that would happen,' I said.

'Who cares for shoes,' said Kiran.

'Who cares,' I said.

I walked back to the veranda and Kiran walked beside me, and stood in front of the hotel while I put my suitcase in the tonga.

'You nearly stayed one day too late,' said the tonga driver. 'Half the hotel has come down and tonight the other half will come down.'

I climbed into the back seat. Kiran stood on the path, gazing intently at me.

'I'll see you again,' I said.

'I'll see you in Iceland or Japan,' she said. 'I'm going everywhere.'

'Maybe,' I said, 'maybe you will.'

We smiled, knowing and understanding each other's importance. In her bright eyes I saw something old and wise. The tonga driver cracked his whip, the wheels creaked, the carriage rattled down the path. We kept waving to each other. In Kiran's hand was a spring of hibiscus. As she waved, the blossoms fell apart and danced a little in the breeze.

Shamli station looked the same as it had the day before. The same train stood at the same platform and the same dogs prowled beside the fence. I waited on the platform till the bell clanged for the train to leave, but Sushila did not come.

Somehow, I was not disappointed. I had never really expected her to come. Unattainable, Sushila would always be more bewitching and beautiful than if she were mine.

Shamli would always be there. And I could always come back, looking for Major Roberts.

*Ruskin Bond*

# the kitemaker

There was but one tree in the street known as Gali Ram Nath—an ancient banyan that had grown through the cracks of an abandoned mosque—and little Ali's kite was caught in its branches. The boy, barefoot and clad only in a torn shirt, ran along the cobbled stones of the narrow street to where his grandfather sat nodding dreamily in the sunshine in their back courtyard.

'Grandfather,' shouted the boy. 'My kite has gone!'

The old man woke from his daydream with a start and, raising his head, displayed a beard that would have been white had it not been dyed red with mehendi leaves.

'Did the twine break?' he asked. 'I know that kite twine is not what it used to be.'

'No, Grandfather, the kite is stuck in the banyan tree.'

The old man chuckled. 'You have yet to learn how to fly a kite properly, my child. And I am too old to teach you, that's the pity of it. But you shall have another.'

He had just finished making a new kite from bamboo, paper and thin silk, and it lay in the sun, firming up. It was a pale pink kite, with a small green tail. The old man handed it to Ali, and the boy raised himself on his toes and kissed his grandfather's hollowed-out cheek.

'I will not lose this one,' he said. 'This kite will fly like a bird.' And he turned on his heels and skipped out of the courtyard.

The old man remained dreaming in the sun. His kite shop was gone, the premises long since sold to a junk dealer; but he still made kites, for his own amusement and for the benefit of his grandson, Ali. Not many people bought kites these days. Adults disdained them, and children preferred to spend their money at the cinema. Moreover, there were not many open spaces left for the flying of kites. The city had swallowed up the open grassland that had stretched from the old fort's walls to the river bank.

But the old man remembered a time when grown men flew kites, and great battles were fought, the kites swerving and swooping in the sky, tangling with each other until the string of one was severed. Then the defeated but liberated kite would float away into the blue unknown. There was a good deal of betting, and money frequently changed hands.

Kite flying was then the sport of kings, and the old man remembered how the nawab himself would come down to the riverside with his retinue to participate in this noble pastime. There was time, then, to spend an idle hour with a gay, dancing strip of paper. Now everyone hurried, in a heat of hope, and delicate things like kites and daydreams were trampled underfoot.

He, Mehmood the kitemaker, had in the prime of his life been well known throughout the city. Some of his more elaborate kites once sold for as much as three or four rupees each.

At the request of the nawab he had once made a very special kind of kite, unlike any that had been seen in the district. It consisted of a series of small, very light paper disks trailing on a thin bamboo frame. To the end of each disk he fixed a sprig of grass, forming a balance on both sides. The surface of the foremost disk was slightly convex, and a fantastic face was painted on it, having two eyes made of small mirrors. The disks, decreasing in size from head to tail, assumed an undulatory form and gave the kite the appearance of a crawling serpent. It required great skill to raise this cumbersome device from the ground, and only Mehmood could manage it.

Everyone had heard of the 'Dragon Kite' that Mehmood had built, and word went round that it possessed supernatural powers. A large crowd assembled in the open to watch its first public launching in the presence of the nawab.

At the first attempt it refused to leave the ground. The disks made a plaintive, protesting sound, and the sun was trapped in the little mirrors, making the kite a living, complaining creature. Then the wind came from the right direction, and the Dragon Kite soared into the sky, wriggling its way higher and higher, the sun still glinting in its devil eyes. And when it went very high, it pulled fiercely at the twine, and Mehmood's young sons had to help him with the reel. Still the kite pulled, determined to be free, to break loose, to live a life of its own. And eventually it did so.

The twine snapped, the kite leaped away towards the sun, sailing on heavenward until it was lost to view. It was never found again, and Mehmood wondered afterwards if he had made too vivid, too living a thing of the great kite. He did not make another like it. Instead he presented to the nawab a musical kite, one that made a sound like a violin when it rose into the air.

Those were more leisurely, more spacious days. But the nawab had died years ago, and his descendants were almost as poor as Mehmood himself. Kitemakers, like poets, once had their patrons; but now no one knew Mehmood, simply because there were too many people in the Gali, and they could not be bothered with their neighbours.

When Mehmood was younger and had fallen sick, everyone in the neighbourhood had come to ask after his health; but now, when his days were drawing to a close, no one visited him. Most of his old friends were dead and his sons had grown up: one was working in a local garage and the other, who was in Pakistan at the time of the Partition, had not been able to rejoin his relatives.

The children who had bought kites from him ten years ago were now grown men, struggling for a living; they did not have time for the old man and his memories. They had grown up in a swiftly changing and competitive world, and they looked at the old kitemaker and the banyan tree with the same indifference.

Both were taken for granted—permanent fixtures that were of no concern to the raucous, sweating mass of humanity that surrounded them. No longer did people gather under the banyan tree to discuss their problems and their plans; only in the summer months did a few seek shelter from the fierce sun.

But there was the boy, his grandson. It was good that Mehmood's son worked close by, for it gladdened the old man's heart to watch the small boy at play in the winter sunshine, growing under his eyes like a young and well-nourished sapling putting forth new leaves each day. There is a great affinity between trees and men. We grow at much the same pace, if we are not hurt or starved or cut down. In our youth we are resplendent creatures, and in our declining years we stoop a little, we remember, we stretch our brittle limbs in the sun, and then, with a sigh, we shed our last leaves.

Mehmood was like the banyan, his hands gnarled and twisted like the roots of the ancient tree. Ali was like the young mimosa planted at the end of the courtyard. In two years, both he and the tree would acquire the strength and confidence of their early youth.

The voices in the street grew fainter, and Mehmood wondered if he was going to fall asleep and dream, as he so often did, of a kite so beautiful and powerful that it would resemble the great white bird of the Hindus— Garuda, God Vishnu's famous steed. He would like to make a wonderful new kite for little Ali. He had nothing else to leave the boy.

He heard Ali's voice in the distance, but did not realize that the boy was calling him. The voice seemed to come from very far away.

Ali was at the courtyard door, asking if his mother had as yet returned from the bazaar. When Mehmood did not answer, the boy came forward repeating his question. The sunlight was slanting across the old man's head, and a small white butterfly rested on his flowing beard. Mehmood was silent; and when Ali put his small brown hand on the old man's shoulder, he met with no response. The boy heard a faint sound, like the rubbing of marbles in his pocket.

Suddenly afraid, Ali turned and moved to the door, and then ran down the street shouting for his mother. The butterfly left the old man's beard and flew to the mimosa tree, and a sudden gust of wind caught the torn kite and lifted it in the air, carrying it far above the struggling city into the blind blue sky.

# the tunnel

It was almost noon, and the jungle was very still, very silent. Heat waves shimmered along the railway embankment where it cut a path through the tall evergreen trees. The railway lines were two straight black serpents disappearing into the tunnel in the hillside.

Ranji stood near the cutting, waiting for the midday train. It wasn't a station and he wasn't catching a train. He was waiting so he could watch the steam engine come roaring out of the tunnel.

He had cycled out of town and taken the jungle path until he had come to a small village. He had left the cycle there, and walked over a low, scrub-covered hill and down to the tunnel exit.

Now he looked up. He had heard, in the distance, the shrill whistle of the engine. He couldn't see anything, because the train was approaching from the other side of the hill, but presently a sound like distant thunder came from the tunnel, and he knew the train was coming through.

A second or two later the steam engine shot out of the

tunnel, snorting and puffing like some green, black and gold dragon, some beautiful monster out of Ranji's dreams. Showering sparks right and left, it roared a challenge to the jungle.

Instinctively Ranji stepped back a few paces. Waves of hot steam struck him in the face. Even the trees seemed to flinch from the noise and heat. And then the train had gone, leaving only a plume of smoke to drift lazily over the tall shisham trees.

The jungle was still again. No one moved.

Ranji turned from watching the drifting smoke and began walking along the embankment towards the tunnel. It grew darker the further he walked, and when he had gone about twenty yards it became pitch black. He had to turn and look back at the opening to make sure that there was a speck of daylight in the distance.

Ahead of him, the tunnel's other opening was also a small round circle of light.

The walls of the tunnel were damp and sticky. A bat flew past. A lizard scuttled between the lines. Coming straight from the darkness into the light, Ranji was dazzled by the sudden glare. He put a hand up to shade his eyes and looked up at the scrub-covered hillside, and he thought he saw something moving between the trees.

It was just a flash of gold and black, and a long swishing tail. It was there between the trees for a second or two, and then it was gone.

About fifty feet from the entrance to the tunnel stood the watchman's hut. Marigolds grew in front of the hut, and at the back there was a small vegetable patch. It was the watchman's duty to inspect the tunnel and keep it clear of obstacles.

Every day, before the train came through, he would walk the length of the tunnel. If all was well, he would return to his hut and take a nap. If something was wrong, he would walk back up the line and wave a red flag and the engine driver would slow down.

At night, the watchman lit an oil lamp and made a similar inspection. If there was any danger to the train, he'd go back up the line and wave his lamp to the approaching engine. If all was well, he'd hang his lamp at the door of his hut and go to sleep.

He was just settling down on his cot for an afternoon nap when he saw the boy come out of the tunnel. He waited until the boy was only a few feet away and then said, 'Welcome, welcome. I don't often get visitors. Sit down for a while, and tell me why you were inspecting my tunnel.'

'Is it your tunnel?' asked Ranji.

'It is,' said the watchman. 'It is truly my tunnel, since no one else will have anything to do with it. I have only lent it to the government.'

Ranji sat down on the edge of the cot.

'I wanted to see the train come through,' he said. 'And then, when it had gone, I decided to walk through the tunnel.'

'And what did you find in it?'

'Nothing. It was very dark. But when I came out, I thought I saw an animal—up on the hill—but I'm not sure, it moved off very quickly.'

'It was a leopard you saw,' said the watchman. 'My leopard.'

'Do you own a leopard, too?'

'I do.'

'And do you lend it to the government?'

'I do not.'

'Is it dangerous?'

'Not if you leave it alone. It comes this way for a few

*Ruskin Bond*

days every month, because there are still deer in this jungle, and the deer is its natural prey. It keeps away from people.'

'Have you been here a long time?' asked Ranji.

'Many years. My name is Kishan Singh.'

'Mine is Ranji.'

'There is one train during the day. And there is one train during the night. Have you seen the Night Mail come through the tunnel?'

'No. At what time does it come?'

'About nine o'clock, if it isn't late. You could come and sit here with me, if you like. And, after it has gone, I will take you home.'

'I'll ask my parents,' said Ranji. 'Will it be safe?'

'It is safer in the jungle than in the town. No rascals out here. Only last week, when I went into the town, I had my pocket picked! Leopards don't pick pockets.'

Kishan Singh stretched himself out on his cot. 'And now I am going to take a nap, my friend. It is too hot to be up and about in the afternoon.'

'Everyone goes to sleep in the afternoon,' complained Ranji. 'My father lies down as soon as he's had his lunch.'

'Well, the animals also rest in the heat of the day. It is only the tribe of boys who cannot, or will not, rest.'

Kishan Singh placed a large banana leaf over his face to keep away the flies, and was soon snoring gently. Ranji stood up, looking up and down the railway tracks. Then he began walking back to the village.

The following evening, towards dusk, as the flying foxes swooped silently out of the trees, Ranji made his way to the watchman's hut.

It had been a long hot day, but now the earth was cooling and a light breeze was moving through the trees. It carried with it the scent of mango blossom, the promise of rain.

Kishan Singh was waiting for Ranji. He had watered his small garden and the flowers looked cool and fresh. A kettle was boiling on an oil stove.

'I am making tea,' he said. 'There is nothing like a glass of hot sweet tea while waiting for a train.'

They drank their tea, listening to the sharp notes of the tailor bird and the noisy, chatter of the seven sisters. As the brief twilight faded, most of the birds fell silent. Kishan lit his oil lamp and said it was time for him to inspect the tunnel. He moved off towards the dark entrance, while Ranji sat on the cot, sipping tea.

In the dark, the trees seemed to move closer. And the night life of the forest was conveyed on the breeze—the sharp call of a barking deer, the cry of a fox, the quaint tonk-tonk of a nightjar.

There were some sounds that Ranji would not recognize—sounds that came from the trees. Creakings, and whisperings, as though the trees were coming alive, stretching their limbs in the dark, shifting a little, flexing their fingers.

Kishan Singh stood outside the tunnel, trimming his lamp. The night sounds were familiar to him and he did not give them much thought; but something else—a padded footfall, a rustle of dry leaves—made him stand still for a few seconds, peering into the darkness. Then, humming softly, he returned to where Ranji was waiting. Ten minutes remained for the Night Mail to arrive.

As the watchman sat down on the cot beside Ranji, a new sound reached both of them quite distinctly—a rhythmic sawing sound, as of someone cutting through the branch of a tree.

'What's that?' whispered Ranji.

'It's the leopard,' said Kishan Singh. 'I think it's in the tunnel.'

'The train will soon be here.'

'Yes, my friend. And if we don't drive the leopard out of the tunnel, it will be run over by the engine.'

'But won't it attack us if we try to drive it out?' asked Ranji, beginning to share the watchman's concern.

'It knows me well. We have seen each other many times. I don't think it will attack. Even so, I will take my axe along. You had better stay here, Ranji.'

'No, I'll come too. It will be better than sitting here alone in the dark.'

'All right, but stay close behind me. And remember, there is nothing to fear.'

Raising his lamp, Kishan Singh walked into the tunnel, shouting at the top of his voice to try and scare away the animal. Ranji followed close behind. But he found he was unable to do any shouting; his throat had gone quite dry.

They had gone about twenty paces into the tunnel when the light from the lamp fell upon the leopard. It was crouching between the tracks, only fifteen feet away from them. Baring its teeth and snarling, it went down on its belly, tail twitching. Ranji felt sure it was going to spring at them.

Kishan Singh and Ranji both shouted together. Their voices rang through the tunnel. And the leopard, uncertain as to how many terrifying humans were there in front of him, turned swiftly and disappeared into the darkness.

To make sure it had gone, Ranji and the watchman walked the length of the tunnel. When they returned to the entrance, the rails were beginning to hum. They knew the train was coming.

Ranji put his hand to one of the rails and felt its tremor. He heard the distant rumble of the train. And then the engine came round the bend, hissing at them, scattering sparks into the darkness, defying the jungle as it roared through the steep sides of the cutting. It charged straight into the tunnel, thundering past Ranji like the beautiful dragon of his dreams.

And when it had gone, the silence returned and the forest seemed to breathe, to live again. Only the rails still trembled with the passing of the train.

They trembled again to the passing of the same train, almost a week later, when Ranji and his father were both travelling in it.

Ranji's father was scribbling in a notebook, doing his accounts. How boring of him, thought Ranji as he sat near an open window staring out at the darkness. His father was going to Delhi on a business trip and had decided to take the boy along.

'It's time you learnt something about the business,' he had said, to Ranji's dismay.

The Night Mail rushed through the forest with its hundreds of passengers. The carriage wheels beat out a steady rhythm on the rails. Tiny flickering lights came and went, as they passed small villages on the fringe of the jungle.

Ranji heard the rumble as the train passed over a small bridge. It was too dark to see the hut near the cutting, but he knew they must be approaching the tunnel. He strained his eyes, looking out into the night; and then, just as the engine let out a shrill whistle, Ranji saw the lamp.

He couldn't see Kishan Singh, but he saw the lamp, and he knew that his friend was out there.

The train went into the tunnel and out again, it left the jungle behind and thundered across the endless plains. And Ranji stared out at the darkness, thinking of the lonely cutting in the forest, and the watchman with the lamp who would always remain a firefly for those travelling thousands, as he lit up the darkness for steam engines and leopards.

*Ruskin Bond*

# a face in the dark

Mr Oliver, an Anglo-Indian teacher, was returning to his school late one night, on the outskirts of the hill station of Simla. From before Kipling's time, the school had been run on English public school lines and the boys, most of them from wealthy Indian families, wore blazers, caps and ties. *Life* magazine, in a feature on India, had once called it the 'Eton of the East'. Mr Oliver had been teaching in the school for several years.

The Simla bazaar, with its cinemas and restaurants, was about three miles from the school and Mr Oliver, a bachelor, usually strolled into the town in the evening, returning after dark, when he would take a short cut through the pine forest.

When there was a strong wind the pine trees made sad, eerie sounds that kept most people to the main road. But Mr Oliver was not a nervous or imaginative man. He carried a torch and its gleam—the batteries were running down—moved fitfully down the narrow forest path. When its flickering light fell on the figure of a boy, who was sitting alone on a rock, Mr Oliver stopped. Boys were not supposed to be out after dark.

'What are you doing out here, boy?' asked Mr Oliver sharply, moving closer so that he could recognize the miscreant. But even as he approached the boy, Mr Oliver sensed that something was wrong. The boy appeared to be crying. His head hung down, he held his face in his hands and his body shook convulsively. It was a strange, soundless weeping and Mr Oliver felt distinctly uneasy.

'Well, what's the matter?' he asked, his anger giving way to concern. 'What are you crying for?' The boy would not answer or look up. His body continued to be racked with silent sobbing. 'Come on, boy, you shouldn't be out here at this hour. Tell me the trouble. Look up!' The boy looked up. He took his hands from his face and looked up at his teacher. The light from Mr Oliver's torch fell on the boy's face—if you could call it a face.

It had no eyes, ears, nose or mouth. It was just a round smooth head—with a school cap on top of it! And that's where the story should end. But for Mr Oliver it did not end here.

The torch fell from his trembling hand. He turned and scrambled down the path, running blindly through the trees and calling for help. He was still running towards the school buildings when he saw a lantern swinging in the middle of the path. Mr Oliver stumbled up to the watchman, gasping for breath. 'What is it, sahib?' asked the watchman. 'Has there been an accident? Why are you running?'

'I saw something—something horrible—a boy weeping in the forest—and he had no face!'

'No face, sahib?'

'No eyes, nose, mouth—nothing!'

'Do you mean it was like this, sahib?' asked the watchman and raised the lamp to his own face. The watchman had no eyes, no ears, no features at all—not even an eyebrow! And that's when the wind blew the lamp out.

# he said it with arsenic

Is there such a person as a born murderer—in the sense that there are born writers and musicians, born winners and losers? One can't be sure. The urge to do away with troublesome people is common to most of us but only a few succumb to it.

If ever there was a born murderer, he must surely have been William Jones. The thing came so naturally to him. No extreme violence, no messy shootings or hacking or throttling. Just the right amount of poison, administered with skill and discretion.

A gentle, civilized sort of person was Mr Jones. He collected butterflies and arranged them systematically in glass cases. His ether bottle was quick and painless. He never stuck pins into the beautiful creatures.

Have you ever heard of the Agra Double Murder? It happened, of course, a great many years ago, when Agra was a far-flung outpost of the British Empire. In those days, William Jones was a male nurse in one of the city's hospitals. The patients—especially terminal cases—spoke highly of the care and consideration he showed them.

While most nurses, both male and female, preferred to attend to the more hopeful cases, Nurse William was always prepared to stand duty over a dying patient.

He felt a certain empathy for the dying. He liked to see them on their way. It was just his good nature, of course.

On a visit to nearby Meerut, he met and fell in love with Mrs Browning, the wife of the local stationmaster. Impassioned love letters were soon putting a strain on the Agra–Meerut postal service. The envelopes grew heavier—not so much because the letters were growing longer but because they contained little packets of a powdery white substance, accompanied by detailed instructions as to its correct administration.

Mr Browning, an unassuming and trustful man—one of the world's born losers, in fact—was not the sort to read his wife's correspondence. Even when he was seized by frequent attacks of colic, he put them down to an impure water supply. He recovered from one bout of vomiting and diarrhoea only to be racked by another.

He was hospitalized on a diagnosis of gastroenteritis. And, thus freed from his wife's ministrations, soon got better. But on returning home and drinking a glass of nimbupani brought to him by the solicitous Mrs Browning, he had a relapse from which he did not recover.

Those were the days when deaths from cholera and related diseases were only too common in India and death certificates were easier to obtain than dog licences.

After a short interval of mourning (it was the hot weather and you couldn't wear black for long) Mrs Browning moved to Agra where she rented a house next door to William Jones.

I forgot to mention that Mr Jones was also married. His wife was an insignificant creature, no match for a genius like William. Before the hot weather was over, the dreaded cholera had taken her too. The way was clear for the lovers to unite in holy matrimony.

But Dame Gossip lived in Agra too and it was not long before tongues were wagging and anonymous letters were being received by the superintendent of police. Inquiries were instituted. Like most infatuated lovers, Mrs Browning had hung on to her beloved's letters and *billet doux*, and these soon came to light. The silly woman had kept them in a box beneath her bed.

Exhumations were ordered in both Agra and Meerut. Arsenic keeps well, even in the hottest of weather, and there was no dearth of it in the remains of both victims.

Mr Jones and Mrs Browning were arrested and charged with murder.

'Is Uncle Bill really a murderer?' I asked from the drawing-room sofa in my grandmother's house in Dehra. (It's time I told you that William Jones was my uncle, my mother's half-brother.)

I was eight or nine at the time. Uncle Bill had spent the previous summer with us in Dehra and had stuffed me with bazaar sweets and pastries, all of which I had consumed without suffering any ill effects.

'Who told you that about Uncle Bill?' asked Grandmother.

'I heard it in school. All the boys are asking me the same question—"Is your uncle a murderer?" They say he poisoned both his wives.'

'He had only one wife,' snapped Aunt Mabel.

'Did he poison her?'

'No, of course not. How can you say such a thing!'

'Then why is Uncle Bill in gaol?'

'Who says he's in gaol?'

'The boys at school. They heard it from their parents. Uncle Bill is to go on trial in the Agra fort.'

There was a pregnant silence in the drawing room, then

Aunt Mabel burst out: 'It was all that awful woman's fault.'

'Do you mean Mrs Browning?' asked Grandmother.

'Yes, of course. She must have put him up to it. Bill couldn't have thought of anything so—so diabolical!'

'But he sent her the powders, dear. And don't forget— Mrs Browning has since . . .'

Grandmother stopped in mid-sentence and both she and Aunt Mabel glanced surreptitiously at me.

'Committed suicide,' I filled in. 'There were still some powders with her.'

Aunt Mabel's eyes rolled heavenwards. 'This boy is impossible. I don't know what he will be like when he grows up.'

'At least I won't be like Uncle Bill,' I said. 'Fancy poisoning people! If I kill anyone, it will be in a fair fight. I suppose they'll hang Uncle?'

'Oh, I hope not!'

Grandmother was silent. Uncle Bill was her stepson but she did have a soft spot for him. Aunt Mabel, his sister, thought he was wonderful. I had always considered him to be a bit soft but had to admit that he was generous. I tried to imagine him dangling at the end of a hangman's rope but somehow he didn't fit the picture.

As things turned out, he didn't hang. White people in India seldom got the death sentence, although the hangman was pretty busy disposing of dacoits and political terrorists. Uncle Bill was given a life sentence and settled down to a sedentary job in the prison library at Naini, near Allahabad. His gifts as a male nurse went unappreciated. They did not trust him in the hospital.

He was released after seven or eight years, shortly after the country became an independent republic. He came out of gaol to find that the British were leaving, either for

England or the remaining colonies. Grandmother was dead. Aunt Mabel and her husband had settled in South Africa. Uncle Bill realized that there was little future for him in India and followed his sister out to Johannesburg. I was in my last year at boarding school. After my father's death my mother had married an Indian and now my future lay in India.

I did not see Uncle Bill after his release from prison and no one dreamt that he would ever turn up again in India.

In fact fifteen years were to pass before he came back, and by then I was in my early thirties, the author of a book that had become something of a best-seller. The previous fifteen years had been a struggle—the sort of struggle that every young freelance writer experiences—but at last the hard work was paying off and the royalties were beginning to come in.

I was living in a small cottage on the outskirts of the hill station of Fosterganj, working on another book, when I received an unexpected visitor.

He was a thin, stooped, grey-haired man in his late fifties with a straggling moustache and discoloured teeth. He looked feeble and harmless but for his eyes which were a pale cold blue. There was something slightly familiar about him.

'Don't you remember me?' he asked. 'Not that I really expect you to, after all these years . . .'

'Wait a minute. Did you teach me at school?'

'No—but you're getting warm.' He put his suitcase down and I glimpsed his name on the airlines label. I looked up in astonishment. 'You're not—you couldn't be . . .'

'Your Uncle Bill,' he said with a grin and extended his hand. 'None other!' And he sauntered into the house.

I must admit that I had mixed feelings about his arrival.

While I had never felt any dislike for him, I hadn't exactly approved of what he had done. Poisoning, I felt, was a particularly reprehensible way of getting rid of inconvenient people. Not that I could think of any commendable ways of getting rid of them! Still, it had happened a long time ago, he'd been punished, and presumably he was a reformed character.

'And what have you been doing all these years?' he asked me, easing himself into the only comfortable chair in the room.

'Oh, just writing,' I said.

'Yes, I heard about your last book. It's quite a success, isn't it?'

'It's doing quite well. Have you read it?'

'I don't do much reading.'

'And what have you been doing all these years, Uncle Bill?'

'Oh, knocking about here and there. Worked for a soft drink company for some time. And then with a drug firm. My knowledge of chemicals was useful.'

'Weren't you with Aunt Mabel in South Africa?'

'I saw quite a lot of her until she died a couple of years ago. Didn't you know?'

'No. I've been out of touch with relatives.' I hoped he'd take that as a hint. 'And what about her husband?'

'Died too, not long after. Not many of us left, my boy. That's why, when I saw something about you in the papers, I thought—why not go and see my only nephew again?'

'You're welcome to stay a few days,' I said quickly. 'Then I have to go to Bombay.' (This was a lie but I did not relish the prospect of looking after Uncle Bill for the rest of his days.)

'Oh, I won't be staying long,' he said. 'I've got a bit of money put by in Johannesburg. It's just that—so far as I know—you're my only living relative and I thought it would be nice to see you again.'

Feeling relieved, I set about trying to make Uncle Bill as comfortable as possible. I gave him my bedroom and turned the window seat into a bed for myself. I was a hopeless cook but, using all my ingenuity, I scrambled some eggs for supper. He waved aside my apologies. He'd always been a frugal eater, he said. Eight years in gaol had given him a cast-iron stomach.

He did not get in my way but left me to my writing and my lonely walks. He seemed content to sit in the spring sunshine and smoke his pipe.

It was during our third evening together that he said, 'Oh, I almost forgot. There's a bottle of sherry in my suitcase. I brought it especially for you.'

'That was very thoughtful of you, Uncle Bill. How did you know I was fond of sherry?'

'Just my intuition. You do like it, don't you?'

'There's nothing like a good sherry.'

He went to his bedroom and came back with an unopened bottle of South African sherry.

'Now you just relax near the fire,' he said agreeably. 'I'll open the bottle and fetch glasses.'

He went to the kitchen while I remained near the electric fire, flipping through some journals. It seemed to me that Uncle Bill was taking rather a long time. Intuition must be a family trait because it came to me quite suddenly—the thought that Uncle Bill might be intending to poison me.

After all, I thought, here he is after nearly fifteen years, apparently for purely sentimental reasons. But I had just published a best-seller. And I was his nearest relative. If I was to die Uncle Bill could lay claim to my estate and probably live comfortably on my royalties for the next five or six years!

What had really happened to Aunt Mabel and her husband, I wondered. And where did Uncle Bill get the money for an air ticket to India?

Before I could ask myself any more questions, he reappeared with the glasses on a tray. He set the tray on a small table that stood between us. The glasses had been filled. The sherry sparkled.

I stared at the glass nearest me, trying to make out if the liquid in it was cloudier than that in the other glass. But there appeared to be no difference.

I decided I would not take any chances. It was a round tray, made of smooth Kashmiri walnut wood. I turned it round with my index finger, so that the glasses changed places.

'Why did you do that?' asked Uncle Bill.

'It's a custom in these parts. You turn the tray with the sun, a complete revolution. It brings good luck.'

Uncle Bill looked thoughtful for a few moments, then said, 'Well, let's have some more luck,' and turned the tray around again.

'Now you've spoilt it,' I said. 'You're not supposed to keep revolving it! That's bad luck. I'll have to turn it about again to cancel out the bad luck.'

The tray swung round once more and Uncle Bill had the glass that was meant for me.

'Cheers!' I said and drank from my glass.

It was good sherry.

Uncle Bill hesitated. Then he shrugged, said 'Cheers' and drained his glass quickly.

But he did not offer to fill the glasses again.

Early next morning he was taken violently ill. I heard him retching in his room and I got up and went to see if there was anything I could do. He was groaning, his head hanging over the side of the bed. I brought him a basin and a jug of water.

'Would you like me to fetch a doctor?' I asked.

He shook his head. 'No, I'll be all right. It must be something I ate.'

'It's probably the water. It's not too good at this time of the year. Many people come down with gastric trouble during their first few days in Fosterganj.'

'Ah, that must be it,' he said and doubled up as a fresh spasm of pain and nausea swept over him.

He was better by evening—whatever had gone into the glass must have been by way of the preliminary dose and a day later he was well enough to pack his suitcase and announce his departure. The climate of Fosterganj did not agree with him, he told me.

Just before he left, I said: 'Tell me, Uncle, why did you drink it?'

'Drink what? The water?'

'No, the glass of sherry into which you'd slipped one of your famous powders.'

He gaped at me, then gave a nervous whinnying laugh. 'You will have your little joke, won't you?'

'No, I mean it,' I said. 'Why did you drink the stuff? It was meant for me, of course.'

He looked down at his shoes, then gave a little shrug and turned away.

'In the circumstances,' he said, 'it seemed the only decent thing to do.'

I'll say this for Uncle Bill: he was always the perfect gentleman.

# the last time i saw delhi

I'd had this old and faded negative with me for a number of years and had never bothered to make a print from it. It was a picture of my maternal grandparents. I remembered my grandmother quite well, because a large part of my childhood had been spent in her house in Dehra after she had been widowed; but although everyone said she was fond of me, I remembered her as a stern, somewhat aloof person, of whom I was a little afraid.

I hadn't kept many family pictures and this negative was yellow and spotted with damp.

Then last week, when I was visiting my mother in hospital in Delhi, while she awaited her operation, we got talking about my grandparents, and I remembered the negative and decided I'd make a print for my mother.

When I got the photograph and saw my grandmother's face for the first time in twenty-five years, I was immediately struck by my resemblance to her. I have, like her, lived a rather spartan life, happy with my one room, just as she was content to live in a room of her own while the rest of the family took over the house! And like her, I have lived tidily. But I did not know the physical resemblance was so close—the fair hair, the heavy build, the wide forehead. She looks more like me than my mother!

In the photograph she is seated on her favourite chair, at the top of the veranda steps, and Grandfather stands behind her in the shadows thrown by a large mango tree which is not in the picture. I can tell it was a mango tree because of the pattern the leaves make on the wall. Grandfather was a slim, trim man, with a drooping moustache that was fashionable in the 1920s. By all accounts he had a mischievous sense of humour, although he looks unwell in the picture. He appears to have been quite swarthy. No wonder he was so successful in dressing up 'native' style and passing himself off as a street vendor. My mother tells me he even took my grandmother in on one occasion, and sold her a basketful of bad oranges. His character was in strong contrast to my grandmother's rather forbidding personality and Victorian sense of propriety; but they made a good match.

So here's the picture, and I am taking it to show my mother who lies in the Lady Hardinge Hospital, awaiting the removal of her left breast.

It is early August and the day is hot and sultry. It rained during the night, but now the sun is out and the sweat oozes through my shirt as I sit in the back of a stuffy little taxi taking me through the suburbs of Greater New Delhi.

On either side of the road are the houses of well-to-do Punjabis who came to Delhi as refugees in 1947 and now make up more than half the capital's population. Industrious, flashy, go-ahead people. Thirty years ago, fields extended on either side of this road as far as the eye could see. The Ridge, an outcrop of the Aravallis, was scrub jungle, in which the black buck roamed. Feroz Shah's fourteenth century hunting lodge stood here in splendid isolation. It is still here, hidden by petrol pumps and lost in the sounds of buses, cars, trucks and scooter rickshaws. The peacock has fled the forest, the black buck is extinct. Only the jackal remains. When, a thousand years from now, the last human has left this contaminated planet for some other star, the jackal and the crow will remain, to survive for years on all the refuse we leave behind.

It is difficult to find the right entrance to the hospital, because for about a mile along the Panchkuian Road the pavement has been obliterated by tea shops, furniture shops, and piles of accumulated junk. A public hydrant stands near the gate, and dirty water runs across the road.

I find my mother in a small ward. It is a cool, dark room, and a ceiling fan whirrs pleasantly overhead. A nurse, a dark, pretty girl from the South, is attending to my mother. She says, 'In a minute,' and proceeds to make an entry on a chart.

My mother gives me a wan smile and beckons me to come nearer. Her cheeks are slightly flushed, due possibly to fever, otherwise she looks her normal self. I find it hard to believe that the operation she will have tomorrow will only give her, at the most, another year's lease on life.

I sit at the foot of her bed. This is my third visit since I flew back from Jersey, using up all my savings in the process; and I will leave after the operation, not to fly away again, but to return to the hills which have always called me back.

'How do you feel?' I ask.

'All right. They say they will operate in the morning. They've stopped my smoking.'

'Can you drink? Your rum, I mean?'

'No. Not until a few days after the operation.'

She has a fair amount of grey in her hair, natural enough at fifty-four. Otherwise she hasn't changed much; the same small chin and mouth, lively brown eyes. Her father's face, not her mother's.

The nurse has left us. I produce the photograph and hand it to my mother.

'The negative was lying with me all these years. I had it printed yesterday.'

'I can't see without my glasses.'

The glasses are lying on the locker near her bed. I hand them to her. She puts them on and studies the photograph.

'Your grandmother was always very fond of you.'

'It was hard to tell. She wasn't a soft woman.'

'It was her money that got you to Jersey, when you finished school. It wasn't much, just enough for the ticket.'

'I didn't know that.'

'The only person who ever left you anything. I'm afraid I've nothing to leave you, either.'

'You know very well that I've never cared a damn about money. My father taught me to write. That was inheritance enough.'

'And what did I teach you?'

'I'm not sure ... Perhaps you taught me how to enjoy myself now and then.'

She looked pleased at this. 'Yes, I've enjoyed myself between troubles. But your father didn't know how to enjoy himself. That's why we quarrelled so much. And finally separated.'

'He was much older than you.'

'You've always blamed me for leaving him, haven't you?'

'I was very small at the time. You left us suddenly. My father had to look after me, and it wasn't easy for him. He was very sick. Naturally I blamed you.'

'He wouldn't let me take you away.'

'Because you were going to marry someone else.'

I break off; we have been over this before. I am not here

as my father's advocate, and the time for recrimination has passed.

And now it is raining outside, and the scent of wet earth comes through the open doors, overpowering the odour of medicines and disinfectants. The dark-eyed nurse comes in again and informs me that the doctor will soon be on his rounds. I can come again in the evening, or early morning before the operation.

'Come in the evening,' says my mother. 'The others will be here then.'

'I haven't come to see the others.'

'They are looking forward to seeing you.' 'They' being my stepfather and half-brothers.

'I'll be seeing them in the morning.'

'As you like . . .'

And then I am on the road again, standing on the pavement, on the fringe of a chaotic rush of traffic, in which it appears that every vehicle is doing its best to overtake its neighbour. The blare of horns can be heard in the corridors of the hospital, but everyone is conditioned to the noise and pays no attention to it. Rather, the sick and the dying are heartened by the thought that people are still well enough to feel reckless, indifferent to each other's safety! In Delhi there is a feverish desire to be first in line, the first to get anything . . . This is probably because no one ever gets round to dealing with second-comers.

When I hail a scooter rickshaw and it stops a short distance away, someone elbows his way past me and gets in first. This epitomizes the philosophy and outlook of the Delhiwallah.

So I stand on the pavement waiting for another scooter, which doesn't come. In Delhi, to be second in the race is to be last.

I walk all the way back to my small hotel, with a foreboding of having seen my mother for the last time.